ADVANCE PRAISE FOR *THE GODS IN SMALL DOSES*

"*The Gods in Small Doses* is the most fun I've had reading in a long, long time. I had that euphoric urge to open my mouth wide, then wider, because something was trapped, a shout or a laugh or a sob, and then they all three burst in like fools through a doorway. This book is so funny, so charming and strange, that I'd follow it into the woods any old evening. Dear Reader, buckle up."

—LINDSAY HUNTER, author of *Hot Springs Drive*

"Mixing the confidence and violence of a Grimms' fairy tale with the sharp perception of the best contemporary critiques of the often senseless ways we work, couple, and live now, *The Gods in Small Doses* is odd, funny, unsettling, timeless, and devastating. These stories will wake you up and keep you awake at night."

—EMMA COPLEY EISENBERG, author of *Housemates*

"I have never eaten god before, but reading Josh Bell feels like coming mighty close. Each story in this collection entered my body like a shocking burst of light. Bell must write with ink given to him by some feral mystic who is guarding an alphabet too hot to touch. *The Gods in Small Doses* is a freaking masterpiece."

—SABRINA ORAH MARK, author of *Happily: A Personal History-with Fairy Tales*

"The stories in *The Gods in Small Doses* are unpredictable and startling little gothic comedies largely about the perversions of childhood and family life—winning, hilarious, and peppered judiciously with breath-catching flashes of emotion washed clean of any overblown sentimentality. Thoughtful, disciplined writing, limning an unknown territory of genre-pleasure that is just short of fabulist: these marvelous stories seem to come from the past and future all at once."

—JORDY ROSENBERG, author *of Confessions of the Fox* and *Night Night Fawn*

THE GODS IN SMALL DOSES

THE GODS IN SMALL DOSES

STORIES

Josh Bell

UNIVERSITY OF MASSACHUSETTS PRESS
Amherst and Boston

Printed in the United States of America

ISBN 978-1-62534-924-8 (paper)

Designed by Deste Relyea
Set in Adobe Caslon Pro and P22 Underground
Printed and bound by Books International, Inc.

Cover design by adam b. bohannon
Cover art by Infinity, *A woman in a black dress.* #973080524 AdobeStock.com.

Library of Congress Cataloging-in-Publication Data
A catalog record for this book is available from the Library of Congress.

British Library Cataloguing-in-Publication Data
A catalog record for this book is available from the British Library.

The authorized representative in the EU for
product safety and compliance is Mare-Nostrum Group.
Email: gpsr@mare-nostrum.co.uk
Physical address: Mare-Nostrum Group B.V., Mauritskade 21D,
1091 GC Amsterdam, The Netherlands

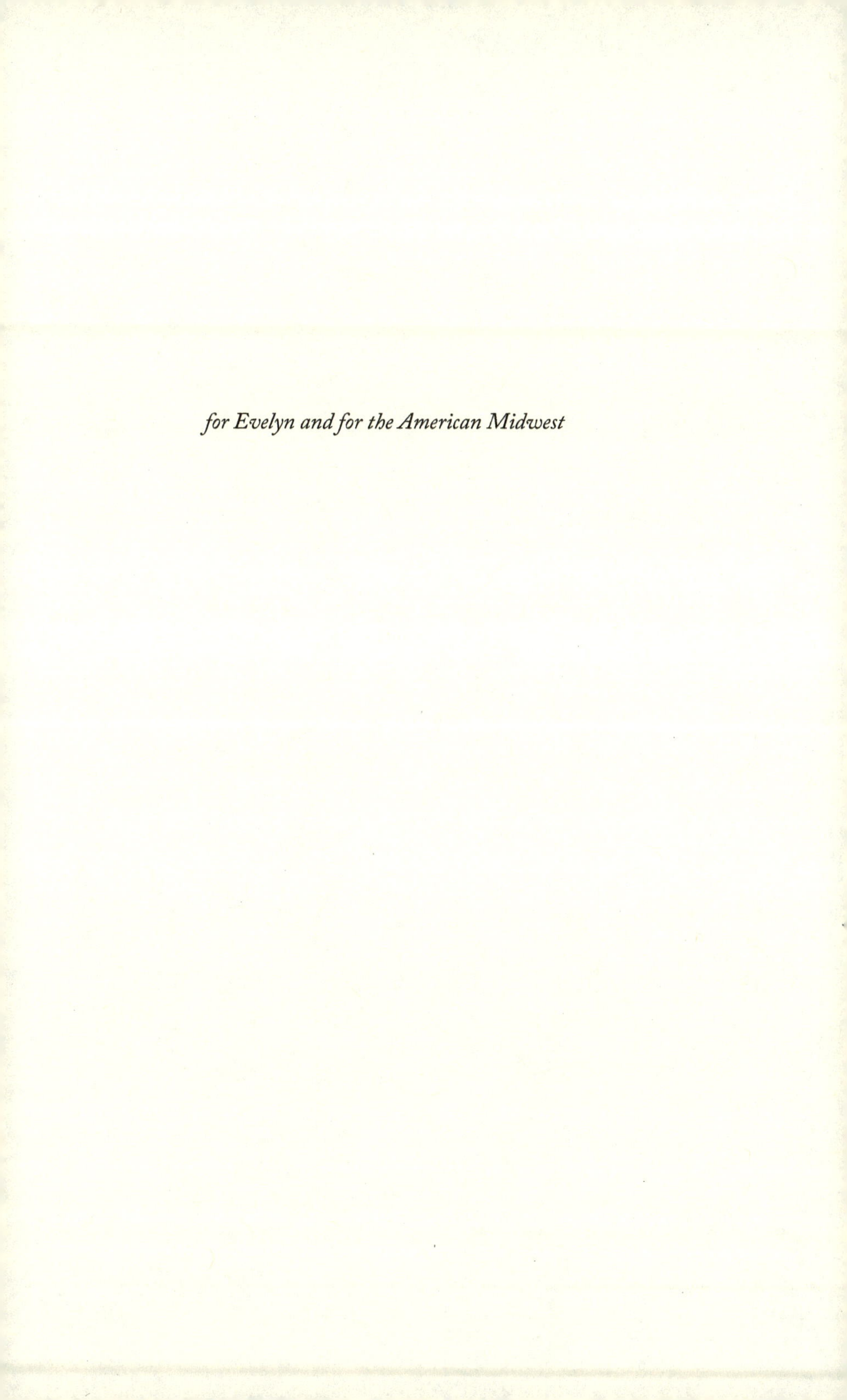

for Evelyn and for the American Midwest

CONTENTS

Have You Heard from Our Assassin? 1

We Hadn't Any Women 5

Easy 25

A Retired Witch 26

We're Always Looking for New Blood 41

Whatever a Ghoul's Supposed to Be 43

Afternoon with Supernatural Orphan 67

The Gods in Small Doses 70

The Ghost of Tracy Valentic 94

Trailer Park Gothic 97

Grant Proposal 110

Death to the Daylight People 111

One Must First Establish a Relationship with the Reader 134

The Regenerating Boy 136

Acknowledgments 161

THE GODS IN SMALL DOSES

HAVE YOU HEARD FROM OUR ASSASSIN?

I ask because, of course, I haven't heard from our assassin.

—

The last time I saw our assassin, according to record, was more than a month ago, Nov. 4th. Evening. By the usual queer means of her preference (messenger rat, a leather collar, a message safety-pinned to the collar, etc.), I summoned our assassin to the Citadel. We met in my offices. She wore a nice black cloak and a scarlet hood I'd never seen her wear before. I asked her to remove her headphones. The messenger rat climbed from the table, up her arm, rested on her shoulder, cleaning its paws. I gave our assassin her instructions regarding the target, said target being the southern witch known to our files as "Sunbeam." Our assassin said she'd heard of the witch Sunbeam. Our assassin said that she heard that the witch Sunbeam was a powerful witch who buried the underclothes of wives and saints in her garden. Our assassin had heard that the witch Sunbeam's garden grew the best tomatoes. I told our assassin the murder of the witch Sunbeam, as far as I could see, seemed a straightforward proposition: I told her she, our assassin, would travel from the Citadel and south through the countryside to the coast, hop a freighter to Canville, enroll in the local high school, get invited to the prom (not a problem for our assassin, as she is a beautiful assassin), assassinate the witch Sunbeam without detection and by whatever means apt, let the body drop on the dance floor, report back to the Citadel to let the Citadel know what song was playing when the witch Sunbeam's body dropped on the dance floor. For an assassin as well versed as our assassin, this Sunbeam killing should have been as simple as the turning off of a light before bedtime. I said that then, and I say it now. And yet now it is almost Christmas, and the prom is long over, and the witch Sunbeam still roams the halls of Canville High, and I haven't heard from our assassin.

—

Have you heard from our assassin?

It has always been the feeling, here in the Citadel, that an assassin is the best tool for the dispatch of witches and heretics. Some prefer to send a priest. Not I. The zeal of a priest makes a priest top-heavy, morally speaking, easy for a witch to topple. But there is no heaviness to an assassin. And there has been no lighter assassin than our assassin.

—

I'm glad to receive from you this letter, containing as it does such useful intelligence regarding the witch Sunbeam's modest rise in power among the peoples of the southern coast, but of course at the same time I'm also disappointed that you, like I, have not yet heard from our assassin.

—

Rumors, signs, unrest. Last night the Canville High Broncos defeated the Citadel 54–48.

—

Though there is some belief amongst soothsayers here, in the Citadel, that we have, in fact, heard from our assassin.

Last night one of the brothers came to me with a strange story. He said he'd just woken from the dream of seeing a green bird. This green bird had flown at him, in his dream. When he opened his mouth the green bird had flown into his mouth and nested in his belly. He'd awakened from this dream with a strange urge to renounce his vows and become a folksinger. I happen to know that this particular brother, in addition to being a bit of an hysteric, is also colorblind.

Do not the colorblind mistake the color green for the color red? Was not our assassin, the last time we saw her, wearing a fetching scarlet hood?

—

We have heard from our assassin.

I awoke this morning to discover a message. The message was a fine silver knife stuck into the outer door of my chamber. The knife was itself the message, I say, since I had given our assassin this very same knife for her birthday the year before last, but this knife also had been used to pin a message to my chamber door. It was a message in the penmanship of our assassin, no mistake, her letters clean, upright as churches. The message read: *Do you even know what a witch is? Canville High rules.*

—

Do I know what a witch is? A witch burns. Do I know what a witch is? What am I to understand from such messagery? That our assassin is now minion of the witch Sunbeam? That innocence is only what I cannot remember? That our assassin and the witch Sunbeam lie on bearskin rugs and do each other's toenails?

—

Have you heard from our assassin?

Let me be more precise about the last time I saw our assassin. Nov. 4th. After I gave our assassin the rundown on the wished-for Sunbeam killing, after I patted the head of the trained rat on her shoulder and passed our assassin the portfolio of particulars and informed our assassin she could equip herself in the armory if she liked (our assassin declined, stating with a certain look in her eye that she was all set on that front), we embraced and said our goodbyes. I would have been distracted by matters of the state for the rest of that afternoon, and so forth, on into the evening. After taking supper I retired to my study, where I read upon books of witchcraft and metallurgy and signed pertinent documents and wrote such memoranda as to be delivered next day to court. Later, feeling restive and wishing to take the night air, I took a walk along the forward alure. While walking I happened to glance over the castle wall and there saw a figure in a scarlet hood moving lightly and surely along the canal, heading south. This of course was our assassin, having exited the Citadel through some postern known only to her and to perhaps a couple of her confederates. I watched our assassin work her way along the canal, the sureness of her pace and the steadiness of her form. I felt glad, when I saw our assassin going about her work with such diligence, that she was our assassin, ours and not some other's. As I watched, our assassin stooped and plucked from the ground what I imagined to be a flower. As I watched, our assassin turned back toward the castle, as if she could feel my eyes on her. She lowered her scarlet hood. You know how our assassin's eyes are. I don't have to tell you. It was too far away and the torchlight along the canal too dim for our assassin to have made eye contact with me, or to have even seen me where I stood, but I felt—there isn't a better word for it—startled by her gaze. So much so that I almost ducked down beneath the battlement so that she couldn't see me. Instead, and perhaps just as stupidly, I raised my hand to her and waved. At my wave she tucked what I supposed to be the flower behind her ear, hooded herself, turned, disappeared into the southern tree line. This was the last time I saw our assassin. I had meant to ask her what bands she'd been listening to recently, to ask her where she'd come across such fine scarlet hooding, to ask her how many confederates she had. It had been a moonless night that night and the battlements dark, very dark. The torchlight along the canal was the only reason I had been able to see our assassin at all. Logic told me that our assassin could not have possibly seen me where I stood upon the battlements, could not possibly have seen me wave to her.

And yet it still hurt my feelings when she did not wave back.

WE HADN'T ANY WOMEN

for Octavia Butler

1

Some of us thought rapture and some of us thought the women simply decided to pack up and leave the island (they were always having secret meetings, these women, down there at the high school gym: little cookies and white wine, tasteful-sex pornography shot onto the ceiling in moving image, fire breathers, lady jugglers boated in special, almost weekly these meetings were, a list of important conversation topics, bobbing for apples; our island wasn't a big island: it had produced, I'd say, thirty to forty women and girls, tops, all fitting easily into the gym, all breathing, talking; and it would've been at just such a gym meeting where the women would have planned their escape, no doubt, *if* escape is what they'd done, if they had not been swept up by God, which is how the older men among us supposed it; God wanted women, this much the old men knew with certainty, no need to think yourself a cuckold when it came to rapture; an old man with his pride will tell you a lot of things when he sits in his attic chair collecting earwax, for example, like how it was always suspected anyway that a woman had been designed for God and not designed for a human man, with the latter's limitations and grim failings, etc., and I listened to what I was told by our old men, sure, just like I was supposed to and like it had been written in the days of yore, but I wasn't so sure what God might have wanted; I mean I had my own ideas about it; I knew a lot about these gym meetings with the women, for instance, which is, number one, that they were fun meetings and that women, in addition to important conversation, liked to have a good time; I am a boy, of course—or else I would not be writing to you about how the women disappeared—but in a dress and a wig I can pass for a girl; sometimes bored and not wanting to hang out long nights with my father building model airplanes in his offices, I would sneak into these all-female meetings at the gym, mainly because I wanted to see what my mother and my sister did when they weren't in the house and weren't around my father, like, when my father wasn't there, I wanted to know who my mother and my sister *were*, if they were, if they existed, which of course they did and did splendidly, and I'd try to sit up in the back of the bleachers so my mother and my sister wouldn't recognize me; it was my mother's wig and my sister's dress I wore as my disguise; it was my sister's high heels and my mother's slip; it was my mother's knee highs and my sister's false eyelashes; what I really wanted to do was wear this black silk number of my sister's that made all the streetlights brighten when she walked outside the house in it, but I knew my sister would recognize this dress on me right away because it was her favorite, so I bit the bullet and always chose one of my sister's lesser dresses, maybe the crepe layabout or the wise sailorette, some garden-variety dress that could conceivably be owned by another girl or even girls, one I hoped my sister wouldn't recognize right off the bat; "Who is that ugly girl back there wearing my dress etc.," I could imagine hearing my sister say, though thank goodness I was never caught, thank goodness my sister never had to think me ugly; but these gym meetings, I'll tell you, they were good-time affairs; they were light and happy and there were often slide presentations; the women always had a lot of information to cover, a lot of info to soak up; and then each meeting ended with the lights in the gym lowered and the women dancing together on the gym floor in bare feet), but no matter how or why the women disappeared, it was definitely certain that the women *were* gone, gone from the island, whether they'd met about it in advance or not, poof, just like that; I remember it was one morning after Christmas, a morning with birds like Vs and Ms in the sky, or you know how it is when the women disappear, how the first women you usually notice as having disappeared are your relatives or the ones who live with you under your own roof, naturally, which is how it was for me that morning, where the first woman I noticed missing was my babysitter, Ohia, who I loved, loved, loved; Ohia!; each night I lay me down to sleep at the foot of Ohia's bed; Ohia was my babysitter of the live-in variety: she spanked you with a pink hairbrush and read to you from gory tales deep into the night; the first thing I would do each morning was stand up from my bedroll at the foot of Ohia's bed and touch her small feet to wake her; Ohia would "humph" and gather me up into her warm arms and pull me close to sleep a little longer, biting on my neck and telling me what a slut I was for mornings; but that morning I woke and found that dear Ohia's small feet were not there, nor was the rest of her body, nor had her bed been slept in; I felt a chill cross my stomach and soon enough—you know it—my father poked his bald head through the door, father with his cock nodding out of his boxers as per usual, like some cross between a bird and a hammer, saying, "These bitches, not again, lord help us," and me saying, "Put your cock up, father," and I walked through the house with my father, our hands on our hips, not finding my mother, not seeing her anywhere, just a memory of the last time I'd seen her, the night before, in the easy chair with her hair stacked up and then slung down at each ear like little bunches of grapes, a book in her hand with foreign words on it and in it, nor was my sister visibly present in the house, my sister with her canine teeth filed down to fangs; she was my big sister, I did love my sister, I did love Ohia, enough that I sometimes got them confused as to who was which, sister or Ohia, particularly when they were in bed together, my sister and Ohia, in bed together where they could be anyone, and the truth is that my mother once told me she wasn't sure whose child I in fact was, and I'd lie awake each night wondering which woman of the three my mother might have been, my mother or Ohia or my sister with her filed-down canines, though none of these women let on if they'd given birth to me or not, not even maybe the neighbor woman Patricia Wilson, Patricia Wilson who sometimes I saw looking out from her window at me while in my bedroom I sat in my masturbation chair, a little wave from Patricia Wilson as she watched me get down to it in the masturbation chair of an afternoon; Patricia Wilson had neat gray hair and no husband, as she was said by men of the island to only make congress with other women of the flesh, and the men would say this about women on women in hushed tones like it was a secret, even though somehow I always just supposed that that's what *all* women did with each other, they seemed to be close together in height in a logical way, but no matter who Patricia Wilson liked to sleep with at night, she did seem curious to watch me in my masturbation chair, clapping her hands together behind her window like she was an audience gathered for me, and I found it cheerful that she did so, it made me feel like an athlete, and I was a boy in that chair while masturbating for Patricia Wilson's enjoyment, and I was a boy when I was not wearing my sister's false eyelashes and my mother's dress, and I was a boy when Ohia would hover over me in the dark at night to see if I was sleeping or lying about it; yes, according to my mother, any woman on the island could have been my mother and given birth to the boy who was me, so that meant Patricia Wilson was a candidate, too, but forever the mystery of who my mother truly was would always be a mystery that I'd never learn, though my father doubtlessly *was* my father (and isn't this always how it is with fathers? so exact? Maybe things are different on your island), no mystery to the man at all nor to me, and now alarmed in his own kitchen my father took phone calls from the other men on the island, standing in the kitchen on flat feet with his cock hanging out all sad about it and saying into the phone to Mikie Rivers (one of our firemen), "Mikie boy, my wife, my daughter, the odd girl Ohia," listing off the names of the missing; then Mikie's nervous voice coming through the phone, "Becka's gone too, she didn't even leave a note, it's not like that time she went to

Cancun," and my father screaming "Note!" into the phone and dashing off to see if my mother or anyone had left him a note, which of course there wasn't any note; it wasn't that kind of disappearance where you're kept informed about the missing women, as most disappearances of women are not, you don't have to tell me about it, with my father now back into the kitchen saying into the phone to the mayor, "Sylvester, my wife is gone, my daughter, even the odd girl Ohia, not even so much as a note," and the mayor saying, "Oh, no, it's happened again," and I stood there and I thought a little bit, and I asked my father, "Again? This has happened before?" and my father cupped the phone and said, "Go talk to your grandfather about it!"

2

So that's what I did; I left the kitchen to my father and his sad dick and the mayor; and with the reach pole I hooked the attic trapdoor and pulled the steps down and I climbed up the steps to talk to my grandfather; of course every house must have an old man in it; and we were lucky to have an old man who was literally related to us; not all households could say the same, for if your related grandfather were to die, then the mayor's office would just send you another old man, an old man to put in your attic, there seemed to be no shortage of old men on our island, though now that I'm thinking about it I'm not sure this old man *was* my literal grandfather, maybe I had just been told he was and believed it; but no matter, as one old man will do as well as another; and anyway there he was in the attic, the purported grandpa, sitting in his easy chair, collecting his earwaxes, counting however many pigeons there were on the powerline that day, and I said, "Grandfather, the women are missing," and Grandfather said, "These bitches, not again?" and I said, "What does that mean, 'again'?" and Grandfather told me all about it: how there was a time when my father had been a boy my age and the women had disappeared, just like this, one morning after Christmas with birds in the sky like Vs and Ms; gone they were, all of the women of the island, my father's mother (my father's mother who was, if you believed this old man in the attic, a woman named Trixie) and also my father's sister, and also my father's live-in babysitter, and then all of the island women in general, just gone; and Grandfather said, "We waited a couple of months, until we believed they were gone forever, and then we did what we had to do, we weren't proud of it. A man is not a woman but he can sometimes be used like one and/or vice versa," and I said, "Grandpa, I don't know that I'm supposed to be told *all* of this story, you old bat," and Grandpa said, "Well what happened was, with the women gone, the men all drew lots. They decided to do it random that way, you know, so that none of us could be accused of having picked out a man he liked in special or to be razzed about having a preference for sideburns or whatever. Your number would match the number of another man in town and you would live together. It took some getting used to. But I was lucky and the man assigned to me (and I to him) was a fisherman and he told wonderful stories about the sea and he didn't mind how I needed to be talked to prior to having my orgasm. I came to love this man and his name was George," Grandpa said, a little tear in the corner of his eye, "but then what happened was, after a while of this, the women just reappeared," and I said, "Your wife Trixie just came back to you?" and Grandpa said, "Yes, she did, your grandmother Trixie and my wife, and she had recently showered, and her hair looked . . . unusual. And all across the island it was true, not just Trixie: the women had come back. They were the same women. Just a little different, more so different than just the hairstyles. I couldn't say *how* they were different, you could just feel it. They didn't say a word about where they'd been and acted like they'd never been gone. A little far-off look in their eyes, maybe, and Trixie herself would stand looking in at the food of the refrigerator for hours on end with that slice of yellow fridge light on her, and the neighbor lady started sunbathing nude on her roof wearing only headphones for her music, little differences here and there, like they knew something they weren't telling you, though, to tell the truth," Grandpa said slyly, "with women, you know, I *always* thought it seemed like they knew something they weren't telling you, whether they had been raptured and disappeared or had just stayed in the same place or not, or maybe it was me that had changed and not them, who can say? And I was happy to have my own true wife back, yes, but I did miss fisherman George. George and I had to split up, you see. There was no room for George and his helpful stories now that the women had returned. It was a very confusing time, dear me, and now it has happened again," Grandpa said; and he sat there quietly, a finger in his ear; and I got mad regarding these facts he had given me, and I said to Grandpa, "You're telling me nothing but lies, old man," and Grandpa was about to chastise me due to my impudence ("impudence" is the word he would have called it), but by this time my father and the mayor and some other luminaries had organized a meeting to be held at the gym, where all hale men of the island would gather together and try to figure out what to do about the fact that we hadn't any women any longer.

3

So I left grandpa in his attic to his pigeon count and I walked over to the gym with my father (who had put some pants on by this time, my father, and I was glad of father in pants, for it bothered me to have to see his naked penis so often nodding from his boxer shorts that way; because though my father's penis was an older penis, the penis of my father looked exactly like *my* penis; it was disconcerting, that resemblance, so typical, so exact; plus, when he was standing on the porch taking in the morning air, or mowing the lawn in the afternoon, the people of the neighborhood could often see this penis, also, and to me it was like people were looking at *my* penis, since our penises looked so much alike; I liked to keep my penis to myself, I didn't like him showing it around, particularly when it came to women seeing it, and—of the women who had formerly been on the island—only my mother, my sister, my babysitter Ohia, and our neighbor Patricia Wilson had seen it, or had seen my version of it, which is only four women out of a total of forty or so, which is a respectably low number for an island like our island, where you keep seeing the same women over and over again and they also keep seeing you) and I walked over to the gym with my father for the meeting, but I could tell right away I wasn't going to enjoy this all-male meeting at the gymnasium as I'd enjoyed other meetings at the gymnasium, where women showed each other slide shows and danced barefoot on the gym floor; no, it was not going to be that kind of meeting; it was a beehive, already the gym pretty full of angry men, shouting at each other, shouting at women who weren't there anymore, the mayor in full dress uniform standing in the middle of the gym floor with a microphone in his hand and having a tough time trying to keep order so that important things about the disappearance could be said; he wasn't doing so well, our mayor, no one was listening to him; like a cat he kept batting his hand against the microphone; I kept my eye on the mayor as my father and I took a seat in the bleachers with the other men, and at this point in the chaos a man the size of a refrigerator named Old Wes strolled from the bleachers out to the mayor, Old Wes taking the microphone from the mayor, Old Wes commanding some authority on this island for his excellent small-engine repair business, the crowd quieting down for Old Wes, and I watched the mayor wilt there on the center of the gym floor to see Old Wes take command, for the mayor may have won their votes, but Old Wes had their respect; people hushed in the audience for Wes; I don't know why

I call them "people"; there were no women any longer, no need for generalities; *men* hushed in the audience; and Old Wes said to us through the microphone, "That's a good question," though I hadn't heard anyone ask a question, and Old Wes continued, "But what I want to know is, is how I'm supposed to feel about it," and some of the men sitting in the bleachers applauded this sentiment, enough men applauding that the mayor in his full dress uniform decided there wasn't much use staying up there like a mayor any longer and he walked over to the bleachers and sat down with the rest of us, and Old Wes continued, the microphone the size of a chopstick in his large hands, he said, "If, as some suppose, the women *have* been raptured, then I know I am supposed to grieve them, and move on, and hope that they might reappear, as they did before, which they might or might not do, again, and, if the old attic men are right, then after we're done grieving, we should draw lots for our new partners, and we will then go about living our lives, maybe a little differently, now, with a strange man to hold hands with and love. But," Old Wes said, "If the women were *not* raptured, if they just left, if they made plans to leave in secret and told no one about it, then don't I have the right, as a man, to be angry?" and the men in the bleachers agreed resoundingly that, yes, in this case Old Wes certainly did have a right to be angry at the women, such women that would meet in secret and plan an escape behind our backs; many of these men stood up and shook their fists, in solidarity with what Old Wes was saying, my father among them, who was angry that his wife and my sister and the odd girl Ohia would take themselves from him, and I'll admit to feeling stirred myself by the words of Old Wes, for when would I next lie on the couch and watch my mother expertly stalking the living room with a flyswatter? and when next would my sister get me high and teach me the String Dance? and when again would the live-in babysitter Ohia choke me to sleep while whispering ancient poetry in my ear?

4

Anyways I know you're reading this to see how I got mixed up with Dave and them at the Female Clinic, and this is how all that happened: with the women gone, and the men closed up in their houses grieving, there wasn't much to do; so to entertain myself—and perhaps to work off some of my anger over being abandoned by the four women I'd loved most in my life (and I do count Patricia Wilson, the neighbor, in this tally)—I took to putting on my sister's and my mother's clothes again; I could feel it had a different meaning now, that I dressed up in these clothes, more ceremonious, for there were no women on the island, none except the boy who put on a wig and false eyelashes and tried his hardest; yes, I took to dressing up, with feeling, sneaking out of the house, wig and all, keeping the spirit alive, then going down to the old gym for dancing, just as the women used to dance in the meetings they held in secret; I did this because I liked the high and lovely feeling of those clothes, yes, but also just because there were a lot of clothes left in the house; wherever the women had gone, they had either packed very lightly or they hadn't packed at all (some of you wonder about me, some of you might ask: you dressed up in your sister's clothes and your mother's clothes, which we understand. But why did you not also dress up in the live-in babysitter's clothes, since you claim to have loved the babysitter Ohia so much? Good question. And the answer: the live-in babysitter, Ohia, only wore one dress. I would have worn Ohia's clothes if there had been clothes for me to wear. Ohia wore one dress, no underthings, no socks, just a yellow floor-length gown, and it was a gown always on her body aside from laundry time, and—wherever it was that she and the other women went when they disappeared from us—dear Ohia had taken her body with her, which meant she had also taken her yellow floor-length gown, which meant that I could not wear it; oh, I would have worn Ohia's lovely yellow gown if I could, dear reader, do not doubt me); and so I stood alone in the center of the gym floor in my sister's sky-blue heartbreak-cut dress or in my mother's black short-stemmed cocktail number and I would conjure up any female energy I could and I would do the String Dance, the dance my sister had taught me, and I would do the Shaky Lamb, which was a dance favored by the live-in babysitter Ohia, and I would do, even, dances of my own invention, the Drunken Marionette, the Fertile Crescent, the Duck, Duck, Wolf; I danced knowing any woman could be my mother and knowing the neighbor Patricia Wilson would not be there to watch me next time I sat down in the masturbation chair; it was a dance of grief; it was a dance of defiance; it was a dance, one night, unbeknownst to me, that a strange man named Dave was watching.

5

I'd worked the horizontal back end of the String Dance so hard that one of my mother's high heels broke and sent me spilling onto the gym floor; I understood then why the women chose to dance in bare feet; and I had loved these black heels of my mother's, they were my favorite of my mother's heels (but isn't that maybe always the way? the mother's black heels, the sexy midnight heels are our favorites and the first to go; maybe it's different on your island), they were so glistening black, these heels, that they looked made out of black licorice, then they formed themselves into dramatic swoops; you would look down at your feet in these shoes and find yourself getting hungry; and now doing the String Dance I had ruined them, they were broken forever; I lay breathing on my back on the gym floor and I let my tears fill up my ears, crying for more than just high heels, and I let myself think of my mother's last hairstyle, the one with it piled up and then slung down to form bunches of black grapes at her ears, and how I used to sit in her lap like an emperor and pretend to pluck from these grapes and eat them, which always made my mother laugh, and I laughed too when I did this, but I laughed only because my mother thought it was funny; I didn't think it was funny; it was not a game for me; I really wanted to eat those grapes that were her hair; it wasn't that I thought they *were* grapes; I knew they were made of her hair and I knew they were connected to her body; this connection, I think, is why I wanted to eat them, to feel the hair unfurl long in my throat and to look up at my mother while she looked down at me; and I lay on the gym floor with the popped heel pressed like a bird to my chest and to my surprise I heard the sound of one person applauding from somewhere in the gym, an echoey sound, a dramatic sound; I raised myself on my elbows and saw a long, thin man walking down the bleachers, across the gym floor, toward me; I had never seen this man before, which is unusual, seeing as how our island is such a small island; the man was a fine figure of a man and he wore a six-piece charcoal suit and he stood over me with his hands on his hips; "You dance with much emotion," the man said to me; he had a smooth-looking face that is tough for me to describe, even now; there were no angles or catches on this face and your eyes just kind of slid off of it without taking anything in; "Thank you," I said to this man, and then he hunkered down so that our faces were at the same level, his face catchless, my face painted like a girl's face, like a sister's; and I asked this man, "Were you applauding for the dance, or because I am crying?" and he said, "For all of it," and he put his light hand on my shoulder and he asked me, "How do you feel about the disappearance of the women?" and he held up a hand when he asked this and he said, "Answer carefully," and so I thought about my answer; and after I thought about it I said, "I am angry at these women, but my anger must travel a long distance through a field of love," and the strange man with the angle-free face widened his eyes and said, "This is an excellent answer," and he produced from the jacket pocket of his six-piece suit a small white card that read:

Dave Charcuterie
Scientist in Waiting
Inventive Pregnancy Division
The Female Clinic

6

Inventive pregnancy is a touch of science and a whole lot of heart; it was part sperm and part dream; inventive pregnancies are not for everyone, I get that, but of all the men on our island, and with so little for them to do with their lives (now that the women were gone) except hold hands with each other and fall in love, nevertheless only two males total volunteered their bodies to the Female Clinic; I was the first volunteer, of course, and I attended the orientation session wearing my sister's church dress (for to the bitter end I am my sister's patriot); it did surprise me, however, that the only other volunteer would turn out to be Old Wes, the small-engine repairman with a head the shape of a bucket, but there walking into the induction room of the Female Clinic was Old Wes himself; I asked Old Wes, "What made you of all people decide to volunteer your body to the Female Clinic?" and Old Wes sat down next to me in the white room, complimented me on the dress I was wearing, and said, "What I grieve most I will become," and I thought then how wise Old Wes was, and I took up his hand in mine and we held hands across the space between us, and now here Old Wes and I were, listening patiently to Dave Charcuterie, Dave C entering the room not in his handsome six-piece charcoal suit but tan slacks and a white shirt and a white lab coat over it, for Dave C, as he was explaining to us now from his smooth face, was a scientist; Dave C said how test-tube babies are one thing, and that of course science can make a baby without trouble and without women, in labs and so forth as we have all seen on television, but what he truly missed was a mother, the mother body, what he truly missed was having women around, like mothers, who have given birth, you love to look at a woman who is a mother, or *had* been a mother, for the look of her is a hopeful look, and not only mothers who had given birth, who had given their bodies up to the child of record, but mainly what Dave C the scientist missed was the sight of a woman, walking around, presently pregnant, heavy with a baby inside her, the fact of generation on the move, or Dave C missed seeing a woman, for example, out of the corner of his eye, reading a book in her fourth month, the belly not fully rounded yet but kind of a promisingly raised flatness, or a young woman dancing, only three months pregnant and not yet too heavy in herself, happy with her life, still feeling young even though—with the gathering of cells and all that heavy carbon—she can't anymore run fast or get away if chased by something toward the woods, but even that helplessness was attractive to the eye, for it is this image of the mother in all trimesters, said Dave Charcuterie, upon which our island civilization has been founded; Dave Charcuterie said, warming to his topic, "For instance I want my mother, right this instant, but she is not here; I want to see my wife's large belly, after I or my brother has made her belly large with our sperm, again and again, and even my brother's wife, Loretta, who deepens into an earthy glow upon her fertilizations, but my wife is not here, and her belly is not here, nor is the belly of Loretta, not unless," said Dave Charcuterie, "I can invent these bellies," and when Dave Charcuterie said this, I could see what he meant; I had looked forward to seeing my sister's belly when great with child in her future and I had looked forward to seeing my live-in babysitter give birth to and care for her own baby and I had even looked forward to being jealous of this future baby of Ohia, since in some ways I myself was also Ohia's baby (no one could say otherwise), and I had looked forward to fighting with a new sibling for Ohia's attention, but now with the disappearance of the women perhaps all this had been robbed from me; and of my mother, who had supposedly given birth to me, all I had was pictures of her pregnant with me for proof, but as my own dear mother had once said to me, when I was sitting on her lap and looking at these pregnant photos with her, said to me low so that my father couldn't hear her, "That's not really you in my belly, I am wearing a falsie," and I had looked at her, and she had said, "Your father got a homeless woman pregnant, and she died giving birth to you," and I didn't believe her about the homeless woman, for my mother had told me many stories about who my true mother was, an astronaut who crash-landed on our island, a gopher woman popped up randy in the front yard, a baseball mitt and a potted plant, but I also believed that my mother—for she was a mother, even just if in name—must have wanted to carry a baby at some point, even if it hadn't been me, and I had dreamed dreams of my mother, comforting dreams of much passion, my mother great with a child who would become my next sister or my first brother, so that I could fight my new sibling for my mother's attention (though what one did with a brother I had not been told and had no idea; would we share clothes? would we have a secret language?); so I thought it possible that being pregnant, me being pregnant, would be like giving birth to my own siblings, that it might be a great blessing on Earth I could give, that such diligence on my behalf and willingness to lay my body on the line might even hasten the return of our women, who would reappear and compliment my industry and thank me for taking the hit for them, and I raised my hand, and Dave Charcuterie winked at me and said, "Do you have a question?" and I said, "It might also be good for morale, too," and Dave Charcuterie smiled and said, "How so?" and I said, "For the men of the island, to see a pregnant belly, it might make them work harder, it might make them happier to know that things haven't changed as much, it might do their little hearts good," and

Dave Charcuterie smiled and said to me, "Of the two volunteers you are my favorite and I will get you pregnant first."

7

Simply put: the uterus was a little black pineapple, inserted through the bellybutton, to be fixed immobile at its center by wire to the spinal column, so that it would hover inside me like, Dave C said, "a little black moon," though it looked to me as I've said like a little black pineapple, though also a "hand grenade," or so said one of the all-male nurses, but I was awake during the procedure, seeing everything, seeing it all, and Dave C and his all-male nurses made sure to show me the device, from all angles, prior to procedure, holding it up in my face so I could see what would be so soon going into me; anyway I watched it off the ceiling viewer, the opening up, the going in; the nurses had hairy knuckles and Dave C kept saying to me, "Keep your eyes on the viewer, this is going to be interesting," and with the silver spreaders the bellybutton on the viewer (which bellybutton was mine) was turned into a sudden lasso; "I feel funny," I said, looking up into the charged pink depths of me, and with forceps Dave C slipped the black pineapple into the bellyhole, which bellyhole seemed to swallow the hand grenade of the womb like a snake would swallow it, and Dave C said to me, "I think you're doing gorgeously, shush now, as I am going to be very near your spine," and Dave C explained to me how the black pineapple already contained an unfrozen female egg and a mix of sperm from seven male donors (only two island men had donated their bodies for fertilization, yes, but the *entire island* donated their sperm; there had been sperm drives; the stainless-steel refrigerators of the Female Clinic were full of the stuff, the seven donors had been chosen at random), and this talk of sperm reminded Dave C of something; he stood back from the operating table; he called for his forehead to be wiped of sweat by two all-male nurses and he said, "Are the fathers here?" and one of the hairy-knuckled nurses adjusted his tricorner hat and said, "I almost forgot," and then the seven fathers, the seven donors, were led into the procedure room to see whose belly they were going into, which was my belly, one after the other these men filed in, masked, each one shaking my hand with a firm grip and calling me mother, the second to the last man resting the palm of his hand on my forehead and saying to me kindly, "Shhh, now little mother, the fathers are here and we love you," and Dave C said, excitedly, "Look how I've made a space for it in the loop of the large intestines, where, once fixed to the spine, the baby will ride, and then over time—and with the growth of the fetus—this simple black pineapple, this hand grenade, this black moon will expand, clearing a space in the boy's middle for a baby to be carried, until he is not a boy but a young mother, and it shouldn't be much longer after that, gentlemen, that we will set this young mother free on the streets of our island city, so that the mother can run errands and read books in public and make phone calls from phone booths, so that we can touch the mother's belly with our hands and week by week we can watch her belly grow."

EPILOGUE

The women returned in my ninth month of pregnancy; they had not been gone that long; it made you wonder, a little bit, why they had disappeared to begin with; but I wasn't about to start questioning them; as a pregnant girl I'd done my share of public appearances—going shopping pregnant, going to the library pregnant, reading a book in the park pregnant, visiting the docks pregnant so that the men could look at me while they loaded cargo—but by the ninth month I'd been confined, by Dave C, to bedrest, in my childhood bedroom, the bedroom I used to share with the babysitter Ohia, though this time it was me sleeping on the bed and not at the foot of the bed; and immediately upon being put on bedrest I'd grown tired of my father waiting on me hand and foot, caressing my belly with assigned lotions and mopping my forehead with a damp cloth and talking to me of news reports (one sad bit of news to relate: Old Wes had miscarried in his third month; something about the yaw of the black pineapple; and since the miscarriage, my father said, Old Wes had let his small-engine repair business fail; "he just can't seem to get interested," my father said sadly, "in making money any longer"), my father hauling in the flowers and candies sent to me by the seven random fathers who had helped make me pregnant, Dusty, Jim, Clarence, Sham, McGee, Manny, and Geoff, all seven of them potential fathers, all sending love and expectation, though it turns out—in other news—that there was also an eighth sperm donor, a secret sperm donor; Dave C stopped by and sat at my bedside with his smooth face; he held my hand and he told me how, last minute, he had added his own DNA to the cocktail that went into the pineapple that went into my belly; Dave C seemed worried I would be angry at him for this forwardness; "I couldn't help it," Dave C said, "I wanted to look at you, like I am looking at you now, and think there was a chance it was my baby making you look the way you look," but I couldn't be mad at Dave C, and I told him how, anyway, whether it be seven or eight potential fathers, it really didn't matter, as I felt symbolically how the whole island was the father of my baby, and Dave C kissed my cheek and told me how understanding and correct I was, and before he left he winked and said something about his sperm being so powerful it could swim to Mars and back; and meanwhile my own father busy in and out of my childhood bedroom with his cock hanging sad from his boxers, the cock looking so much like the fact of my own cock, though I have to admit that it was kind of a relief to see it, in truth, since with the swelling of my belly it had been so long since I'd lain eyes on my own, and then (of course) my father bursting in one morning to tell me how the women had returned, which made me feel joy; even though I had been so mad at these disappeared women, when they reappeared on that bright fall day with birds like Vs and Ms in the sky, I was glad to see them; my mother was the first to visit me, and she pointed at my belly and said, "I can see you've been busy," and she leaned down over me and said into my face, "I'm so glad you got this chance to be a mother, whereas I never had the honor of being a mother myself," and I said to my mother, "*You* are my mother," and my mother laughed and tousled my hair and said, "You wish," and then my sister came into the room and touched her tongue to one of her sharpened canine teeth and she said, "You can borrow my dresses anytime, honey, once you get your body back; I have a hot new one with an exposed back that I think you'll like," and I wondered where my sister had been to have found such wonderful-sounding dresses, and even the neighbor Patrica Wilson came into the bedroom, for she had heard the news of my pregnancy, too, and though Patricia Wilson didn't stay long she touched my bare foot and she said, "As soon as you deliver, I hope to see you in the masturbation chair again," and I assured Patricia Wilson I would try, and (a little overwhelmed) I told the room how I had not been masturbating much, now that I was carrying a baby, because I feared the strange things that I thought during such moments would somehow transport into the baby's head, and everyone in the room laughed at this idea, and I sat there looking up at these faces looking down at me, and I could even hear old Grandpa up in the attic stomping his feet in celebration, shouting, "A baby, a baby, just like in the old days," and my mother shouted at my grandfather to shut up and count his pigeons, which caused a shriek from my grandfather because he had not yet been told that the women had returned, and then my bedroom door opened again, and in came the babysitter, Ohia; Ohia in her yellow floor-length gown!; I had not forgotten Ohia, nor she me; I loved her still; when I asked her where she had been, she whispered something, something I could not hear, to my sister, and both my sister and Ohia laughed, and Ohia put her arm around my sister, and even though they weren't telling me their secrets it was nice to see the two of them, my sister and Ohia, standing so close to each other once again, to just put my eyes on them and wonder if either were my mother and which one was my sister; but there was no doubt, no doubt at all, that Ohia—no matter who else she might be—was still my babysitter, because then her face grew stern and she directed everyone out of the bedroom; Ohia would take care of me now, she would see me through the final month and the delivery; she clapped her hands and everyone filed out of my childhood bedroom, saying well-wishes over shoulders, and when they were gone Ohia pulled up a little stool bedside and sat down; she put her small palm on the swell of my belly; she said, "You have the power to give life, which makes me very grateful to you," and I said, "Ohia, I missed you," and Ohia pulled her pink hairbrush from the drawer of the nightstand and she said: "Your baby will be a strong girl baby and then I will name her Ohia."

EASY

No one's going to burn. No one's going to set you on fire and burn you. No one's going to set themselves on fire, and no one's going to drive too fast. No one's going to run you down. No one's going to abduct you. No one's going to abduct you, no one is going to force you. No one's going to turn your family and friends against you. There'll be a violence, perhaps a light dismemberment. There will be too many men, and there will be too many women. There will be the dead, but there will not be a death, there will not be dying. No one's going to kill you is what I'm trying to say. Who said no one's going to kill you? No one's going to kill you, nor stop you from living. No one's going to kill your family or friends. No one is listening. Your parents aren't listening and no one is listening to your parents. Your children aren't listening and everyone is listening to your children. There may be guns, there may be knives. There will be books, and not just the Bible. There will be states, there will be governments, there may be a cult, there will be cult members. There may be a marriage and there might be a hell. No one said there might be a hell. No one's going to send you to hell. No one's going to send you to the bank, nor will anyone go to the bank for you. No one's going to fall in love with you when you walk into the kitchen in the morning nor when you walk into the campfire light at night. Neither will anyone feed you a poison. This is one thing I wanted to be sure to say: no one's going to feed you a poison, nor leave you face up in a ditch, nor read you a story, nor put you (nor sing you) to sleep.

A RETIRED WITCH

This was an old woman who had been called a witch. She chewed plug tobacco and made craft poisons in her kitchen. She wore a canary-yellow dress most days and most days she drank tub whiskey. She kept a threesome of goats—for the fur and the companionship—in an old tri-bar pen out near the barn behind her peeling farmhouse.

—

That morning the old woman went out to the tri-bar goat pen with a bucket of feed for the goats, clicking her teeth and calling her critter call. The old woman meant to be drunk and she was. The old woman's critter call went "Whoop you goats." "Whoop you goats!" the old woman called, and the food in the bucket was a good food for the goats, to put a rich shine in their fur and a thrum in their dark little hearts. But this morning, as it happened, the goats didn't answer.

—

When the old woman got to the tri-bar fence she could count only two goats in the pen, not the usual three. Only two, the females, spooked and shying from a blood trail in the hay that led from the tri-bar pen, through the grass, toward the hills. The blood shone metallic in the morning sun. The old woman looked at the blood and then she looked at the two goats. No matter how hard she looked at the goats they would not add up to more than two. It was the male goat missing. Something had either murdered it and carried it off or carried it off and murdered it.

—

Even with the good-smelling bucket of feed in her hand the two does wouldn't come near the old woman. She had to sit herself down on the edge of the water trough and talk to them rationally. Eventually the one with the periwinkle blush of fur on its tummy walked its stilt walk over to the old woman. The periwinkle butted its head against the woman's knee and nibbled at the hem of the old woman's canary dress. The old woman scratched the underside of the periwinkle's chin and said: "What carried off your old man?"

—

In the kitchen the old woman sipped a little tub whiskey and she vialed up some poison she would sell to the clerk of the general store. She unhooked her white sunhat from the wall peg and set it on her head, where—she had to admit—it didn't feel right. She took the white sunhat off, looked at it. Then she turned it around and put it on again, this time frontways.

—

The old woman had two stoves, one for cooking the stews that she froze and ate for herself during the winters, the second stove for the cooking of the poisons she sold in town. In between the two stoves was a scarred kitchen table and the old woman stood next to it in her canary dress and white sunhat. She had, even now, some poisons bubbling on the second stove. The poison in the tall black pot, for example, had been simmering slowly for about a month straight. Some poisons took longer, some poisons took less long. The old woman stirred the poison in the tall black pot and then she turned to check the second stove, not the poison stove, but the food stove, where a nice beef stew had been cooking. It was important not to confuse the stoves and the old woman never did. The old woman lowered the flame beneath the stew and she collected her handbag. She put the poison vials, the ones she meant to sell, into the handbag. She wondered if maybe while she was in town she should see about buying another goat, but at last she thought it best to wait until she'd dealt with whatever had carried off her missing goat to begin with. No need to keep handing goats over.

From a lavender sachet she popped a mushroom-looking plug of tobacco between her cheek and gum and she set out of the house and walked out to the dirt road that led to the nearby village.

—

On her way to the village the old woman thought about the missing goat, the male, who had been a good goat. She had nutted that goat when he was a buckling and he had never even looked crosswise at her. He had been a wise leader and with his hooves he sometimes scraped up worms and grubs for himself and the does to eat, standing off politely for the does, beard trembling as he worked his jaws. There had been no mountain lions or wolves in this country for some time. Coyote, maybe, or dog. A hungry-enough dog could carry off a goat, sure, but the old woman believed that, in the night, she would've been awakened by what a dog would do. A dog would get confused as to whether killing a goat was business or fun and this might be likely to lead to an uproar. But the old woman had heard nothing all that night. It was perplexing. She had kept goats for a number of years and she had never lost a goat this way.

—

The poison the old woman sold in the village that afternoon was the poison she cooked up regularly, from a base of ferret weed, nothing special. The woman called this poison Sweet Prince. Sweet Prince was an easy poison to craft and it sold very well. The clerk was happy to get his hands on the Sweet Prince but he was interested in other flavors.

"Got any of that fine poison you sold me last winter?" the clerk asked the old woman. The clerk was a younger man who wore a green visor and whose teeth curved inwardly like sickles. His father had been an older man who wore a green visor and whose teeth curved inwardly like sickles, but this father was dead now.

"Remind me," the old woman said.

"It was a bluish concoction," the clerk said, "and it worked quite swiftly, and it didn't smell like anything."

"Doom Bloom," the old woman said.

"Yes," the clerk said, tapping his visor with the tip of his pencil, "The Doom Bloom."

"Just Doom Bloom," the old woman said.

"Doom Bloom, yes. I sold out of it. It was a popular one. Gophers and stepmothers were dropping like flies all around the county."

"Doom Bloom is out of season, I'm afraid," the old woman said.

"Well," the clerk said, "keep me in mind."

"I will," said the old woman, and then the old woman told the clerk about the missing goat and the blood trail.

—

"A wild boy," the clerk said.

"A what?"

"You're not the first," the clerk said. "The Porters down the way lost a sheep. The Joneses down the other way lost any number of chickens. And then the Wilsons."

"What about the Wilsons?"

"Old man Wilson is the one who saw it," the clerk said, glad the old woman had asked. He leaned on the counter. Behind him stood, on shelves, an army of canned goods, beans green and beans brown. "Old man Wilson heard a calf crying in the night. He got his shotgun and he went out to the fence line. What he saw was a wild boy with its teeth in the neck of a calf, half riding it, half trying to drag it off."

"A wild boy," the old woman said.

—

Back at the farmhouse the old woman led the two remaining goats from the pen and set them loose in the backyard for a spell to give them some room to stretch their legs. The old woman sat up on her back porch and rested and thought about the wild boy and she watched the goats in her yard. As usual the goats didn't know what to do with their freedom. They stood for a while beneath the old shade tree near the goat pen. They walked their stilt walk to the porch steps and looked up at the old woman. After staring at the old woman for a bit, the periwinkle led the other female right back to the tri-bar pen. Once inside, the periwinkle turned around and stuck her head through the fence and looked at the old woman questioningly. The old woman stood and went into the house for a pail of the good-smelling goat feed.

—

Toward dusk the old woman had an idea. She staked the two goats in the corner of the tri-bar pen nearest the barn and she gave them about four feet of tether. The periwinkle tested the tether and so did the other goat and both goats protested.

"Hush, now," the old woman said to the goats.

—

After staking the goats, the old woman walked across the pen, through the gate, and over to the barn. It had been a long day already and sadly the old woman had been sober for most of it. In a corner of the barn, under some old cheesecloth, she found the wolf traps she was after, oily and closed-mouthed. When she leaned over to inspect the traps, her white sunhat tumbled off her head—she'd forgotten she was wearing it—and onto the floor of the barn. She picked up the sunhat and fixed it back to her head and then she took it off and she turned it around the right way and then she stood there looking at the traps. They looked like new. The wolf traps had been oiled and left there by a man named Robertson more than thirty years ago, back as far as when the old woman had not been an old woman. For a time the old woman had shared a bed with the man named Robertson, but she didn't remember that much about him, other than Robertson had complained about the old woman's habit of sleeping without her nightclothes on, which he thought unseemly. That and how the man Robertson had enjoyed a drink the same as the old woman, but thought the habit of drinking, at least in the female of the species, a sign of loose moral character.

—

Now the old woman sat on the dirt in the middle of the pen, the three wolf traps in front of her. She listened to the stop and start sound of a cropduster flying somewhere nearby. From a vial and with a nailbrush she was painting poison onto the teeth of the wolf traps. She looked up from this work and she saw a nuthatch peeking out at her from behind the shade tree across the way, the sun red in the hills behind it. The nuthatch flicked around behind the tree and peeked out at the old woman from the other side of the tree, like he needed to have another look at her. The old woman looked down at what she was doing. Then she looked up and spoke to the nuthatch.

She said, "It doesn't make sense to me either."

—

The poison the old woman selected for this job was the poison called Down Time. Strained carefully and diluted with tap water, Down Time wasn't a fatal poison. When she had trouble sleeping the old woman had even used Down Time on herself. The old woman sipped from her flask of tub whiskey and sat in the pen and painted diluted poison onto the tooth of each trap, dipping her brush into the vial, careful not to get any on her fingers. It took her some time to do so. The sun disappeared behind the hills. The two goats stood quietly at the edge of their tether and watched the old woman work like she was a performer come to put on a show for them.

—

In an arc a couple of feet further than the goats could step, the old woman set the three painted wolf traps. Say what you will about the man Robertson, but he had stored his traps well. They opened easily and they set with no bother. She scattered hay over the traps, careful not to trigger them. She stood back and looked to see what it looked like. It looked exactly like someone had carefully tried to hide wolf traps under hay in her goat pen. It was too late in the evening to dig the traps into the dirt to make them less obvious, which the old woman realized she should have done to begin with. So she scattered hay here and there, all over the pen, to make the appearance of hay in the pen look somewhat natural. She spoke harshly to this hay when the hay didn't fall where she meant for it to fall. She hoped this didn't all wind up with her trapping a stray dog or one of her own goats. She looked at the two goats and she burped from tub whiskey and she said, "Let's find out how stupid this wild boy is."

—

Later the old woman sat in a chair just inside the kitchen door and she drank tub whiskey from a flask and she had a good view of the goat pen. She kept the long gun, loaded, across her lap. For a drunk old woman, she kept good lookout, even if she did say so herself. She read a little from magazines while she waited. She looked at some mail-order pornography.

—

The magazines the old woman favored were magazines in which strange women, not necessarily witches, talked about different kinds of poisons they'd crafted. The pornography the old woman favored was a pornography that depicted nude men in the act of parasailing. She had never been parasailing herself, nor seen an ocean, but she liked the idea of it and she liked looking at the pornography. She sipped at the whiskey and she looked at photos of young men in parasailing rigs and she looked out over her tri-bar goat pen. She fell asleep in her chair. It had been many years since there had been a wild boy loose in the hills.

—

Not that night did the wild boy come, nor the next night, but the third. By this time the old woman had dug her traps in about three inches. She sat on the same chair just inside the kitchen door, her white sunhat like a moon on the wall peg behind her, and as she watched, she saw the wild boy approaching the pen. The old woman did not quite believe what she was seeing and she blinked her eyes. "Here we go," the old woman said.

—

If the wild boy had ever worn clothes, he was not wearing clothes now. The wild boy did not move on all fours, like the old woman had thought he might, but crept slowly on two feet, nearly like a human. Even in the moonlight the old woman could tell the wild boy's hair was a golden yellow. It was ratted and caked with filth and goat blood, but it was yellow. Outside of magazines the old woman had not seen yellow hair before. She was a brunette herself (when her hair had had color) and she'd lived all her life near a brunette village. But this wild boy was blond and he moved slowly, hunched over, his upper body parallel to the ground. The periwinkle goat stood and the other goat took notice and both goats began to warn each other about the intruder. The wild boy climbed over the tri-bar fencing and he did not look left or right, but moved directly, in a crouch, toward the periwinkle goat, who was the pick of the goats. The old woman watched it all. The wild boy stepped into the mouth of the center-most trap, perfectly, like it had been drawn in an illustration. The old woman feared he might collapse headlong into one of the other traps, but he didn't. The wild boy fell down on his back and he howled.

—

By the time the old woman got herself to the pen the Down Time poison was already working on the wild boy and the howling had turned into a mutter. The wild boy lay on his back muttering and he stretched out like he would just sleep that way with his foot in a trap in the moonlight as long as anyone didn't mind it. The muttering turned to little dove-like coos. The old woman stood over the wild boy and looked down. The wild boy wouldn't look at her. She could see that his body, also, was covered with a light golden fur. She lowered the nose of the long gun at the wild boy in case the wild boy knew what a long gun was. He didn't seem to know what a long gun was. The wild boy touched the nose of the gun with a finger and closed his eyes.

The old woman said, "You killed my goat."

—

The two she-goats didn't like how there was a wild boy in the pen with them and the old woman wasn't sure what to do with the wild boy now that she had him. Why hadn't she killed him outright? The old woman wondered about this. It would have been the easiest thing in the world to have coated the teeth of the wolf trap with a fatal strength of Down Time or with any one of her deadlier poisons, but she had not done so. It would be easy, right now, to touch the nose of the long gun to the wild boy's forehead and end it that way. But she found that she didn't want to do this either, particularly now, with the wild boy in the dust of the goat pen at her feet. She liked what color she could see of the wild boy's ratted hair. She knew very well that you could not keep a wild boy, but neither did she want to be responsible for killing the last of something.

—

"Therefore you have arranged this problem for yourself," the old woman said. She said this to herself and she sat down on the hay next to the body of the wild boy and she rested the barrel of her long gun across the wild boy's chest. She leaned over the wild boy's body and lifted one of his eyelids and saw that the eye was blue. She *had* seen blue eyes before. She wasn't a yokel. She ran her hands over the wild boy's chest to feel the consistency of the yellow fur that grew fine and matted on his body. The genitalia between the wild boy's legs was covered in the same fur and the old woman didn't look very long at it. The boy had no real beard to speak of, again just the fine, light fur covering the cheeks and chin, like down. He was a wild boy, after all. The old woman wondered if the wild boy had ever had a home or knew a language. From the looks of him she doubted it. What you could see of his teeth was not a happy story. She sat there and she thought and she watched the wild boy's breathing raise and lower the barrel of the gun she'd set across his chest. After a while the old woman lifted her long gun and she stood in her canary dress. With sticks she triggered the two remaining wolf traps. She led the two she-goats by tether from the goat pen and she locked them over in the barn and she walked in the dark back up to the farmhouse.

—

The old woman made several trips back and forth to the farmhouse. The moon was the one that looked like the horns of a snail. In the pen the old woman assembled the following items: a lantern, a bar of greenish soap and some towels, a pail, a couple of more vials of Down Time (in case the wild boy should begin to stir), a medicine bag, a square of used plywood, and some bandages. She stood and looked over the items to see what she might have forgotten. She looked at the wild boy. Once more she returned to the farmhouse and when she came back she carried with her a silver pair of long-stemmed scissors and in her other hand she held the white sunhat by the brim.

—

The old woman stuck a plug of tobacco between her cheek and gum and she leaned the long gun against the tri-bar fence. She turned and looked at the wild boy, dead to the world. The goats over in the barn didn't like the dark of it and the old woman could hear one of the goats bleating and butting its head against the barn door. "That'll be the periwinkle," the old woman said to the wild boy.

—

The old woman had hung the white sunhat on the gate pole of the pen and she turned and lifted up the sunhat now. She stood over the body of the wild boy and leaned down easily and she positioned the white sunhat over the wild boy's genitals, for his modesty, she guessed, though she wasn't certain. It had seemed like the thing to do and it's why she'd brought the sunhat from its wall peg in the kitchen in the first place, though the old woman had to admit that, when she looked down at the wild boy, naked and gold with a white sunhat covering his genitals, modesty hadn't been the effect, exactly. Now it looked more like he was posing.

—

The old woman stood there not knowing if she would laugh about the sunhat or not and she finally did and she drank from her flask of tub whiskey. She looked down at wild boy's trapped leg and she brought the lantern over and the medicine bag. The teeth of the trap had closed low on the wild boy's calf and though it looked ugly the old woman didn't think there were any problems with the bone. She set the lantern there close to the leg. She spat tobacco juice on the hay between the wild boy's feet. She leaned over and got her fingers between the teeth of the trap and she pulled.

—

With the wild boy's leg cleaned and bandaged the old woman scooted the square of plywood beneath the wild boy's head and then she stood and turned and drug the water trough from its place at the fence edge so that it paralleled the body of the wild boy. More stars had joined up with the moon, and the sky seemed high up on tentpoles above her. She saw how the water in the trough bore bits of swollen goat feed, dead leaves. Even so, it was cleaner than the wild boy's hair.

—

She stepped across the wild boy's body and she sat down on his chest like his chest was a saddle and she dipped her pail into the trough and poured the water over the wild boy's head and she used the green soap. It was an involved head of hair and it smelled rank and living and as she washed it she watched what fell from it, husks of cicadas, chicken bones, mud-dauber nests, a flattened tin can, what looked to be a human bicuspid, sticks and twigs and burrs, a small red rubber ball, a rusted necklace, a treble fishhook, three rusted twist ties, an old pill bottle, here and there a smattering of buckshot plinking out like diamonds onto the plywood board. It was not pleasant work, dying fleas rising up in the lather, but as she washed the hair the old woman grew happy to see the gold color of the hair brighten and deepen. She'd rise and fall lightly with the wild boy's breathing and she'd work the green soap to a lather between her hands and then work it into the hair of the wild boy. She'd lift a length of it, heavy like a fish, and pour trough water over it, then work the greenish soap into it again. It was best to work length by length. That way you didn't get overwhelmed. At first the hair felt thick like tar but after a while it began to plump and spread. The wild boy yelped a little in his sleep, a dream of farmers and chickens, maybe even of goats. The old woman stood up and fetched a vial of Down Time and droppered some onto the wild boy's lips.

—

It was a moldy mattress nibbled by mice and it had been the old woman's marital mattress more than forty years ago, back when the old woman was not an old woman, back when she had been married, not to the man Robertson, but to a different man altogether, a man whose name the old woman had taken as her own for a time, a name she couldn't, just now, quite remember. This man to whom the old woman had been married: he had called her a witch very often and he favored making love through a hole in a sheet, if at all. He did nothing but walk the forest edge and sketch weed flowers. Later she would watch this man burning his own weed flower sketches in the firepit and wonder who in the world he was. She had been a teenager then. Everything had made sense in her head but rarely would anything outside her head match up with what was inside. When this man her husband had died (in his sleep it was said, though some said poison) the old woman had happily replaced the cornhusk mattress with one of fine goose down and she had stored the cornhusk mattress in the cellar. Now the old woman drug this very cornhusk mattress up from the cellar. It was not a heavy mattress but it was hard work to get the old mattress up from the cellar in the dark, to get the mattress out into the backyard in the night, to drag the mattress to the goat pen, harder still to roll the wild boy's unconscious body onto the mattress, but she had done it, nipping tub whiskey from a flask for strength, talking to herself of her own foolishness.

—

The old woman took one last trip to the farmhouse. She was well drunk by now and she felt she had worked off the last of the cartilage in her skeleton and her bones felt unrelated to each other. In the bathroom she sat down to make water and nearly fell asleep while doing so. In her bedroom she located a little jarlet of honeysuckle perfume with which she meant to perfume the wild boy's hair. In the chest at the foot of her bed she found the strawberry and mint quilt with which she would cover the wild boy's sleeping body. In the kitchen she ladled out a large amount of hot stew into a pail and she took these things with her out to the goat pen.

—

The old woman set the pail of stew next to the cornhusk mattress upon which the wild boy lay on his back, unconscious, the white towel bonneting his hair, the white sunhat covering his genitals. The old woman knelt next to the mattress and she unwrapped the towel from the wild boy's head and she dried the golden hair with the towel, holding the heaviness of the boy's head between her palms. She spread the hair out on the mattress around his head so that it might dry faster. From the jarlet she sprinkled some of the honeysuckle perfume into this hair. She stood up with the strawberry and mint quilt and she flapped it over the wild boy's body and let it fall over him. She reached beneath the quilt and brought forth the white sunhat and she hung the sunhat on the gate pole. And she stood there for a while looking at the arrangement. Then, thinking of something, she picked up the lantern and turned and walked out of the goat pen and crossed her backyard, turned at the old shade tree, walked around a little, the lantern lowered in front of her, scanning the grass here and there with her eyes. She knelt in the grass and plucked from it a couple of small white weed flowers. She stood and brought the flowers with her back into the goat pen. She knelt and balanced the two weed flowers by the stems along the mouth of the stew pail.

—

Lastly she took the silver pair of long-stemmed scissors and she bent and cut a lock of the wild boy's golden hair. She figured the wild boy would run before morning, so she wanted a souvenir. She held the lock of hair up before her eyes in the moonlight and she looked at it and then she tucked it into the pocket of her canary dress. She was too tired, by now, to gather up the rest of her things. She made sure to bring her long gun and the scissors, anything with which the wild boy might hurt himself or her when he awoke. She patted the pocket of her canary dress for her flask of tub whiskey and it was there. She walked across the yard and up to the porch and in by the kitchen door. She drank a glass of water at the sink and she ladled some stew into a bowl for herself and she took it out to the porch with her so she might watch to see what the wild boy would do.

—

She figured the wild boy would run, but she meant to stay awake until morning if she could—to see how the wild boy would act when he woke up, to see how the wild boy felt about a bed for himself and a flower for his stew—and the old woman did stay awake for a while, looking out across the backyard at the white halo of her sunhat on the gate pole of the tri-bar pen, the glint of the wild boy's hair in the moonlight, yellow like a fire that couldn't burn anything, his chest rising and falling. The old woman touched at the lock of hair in the pocket of her canary dress and she talked to herself a little and she did not think about the man Robertson nor the man to whom she had been married once, if briefly. She nipped at the flask of tub whiskey and she made sure to keep her long gun across her lap. She fell asleep for a long time and she dreamed of herself as a girl. In the dream her hair was somehow yellow and she had much strength in her legs and she performed strange miracles with the power in them.

WE'RE ALWAYS LOOKING FOR NEW BLOOD

You're a good-looking kid and all the androids want to fuck you. Why not get paid for it?

—

I see six androids in this place, right now, undressing you with their eyes. You're so hot. You're so blood-bearing.

—

That you breathe, that you heal, that you sigh, that you laugh, that you look up at the moon when you take out the garbage, that you write a poem with a little animal in it, that you say a prayer for your mother, that you look so hot, that you need money.

—

Also: you like movies that make you think. You like to shave your body. You might like, one day, to have children. You believe in angels. You read books and you own a pet. You were given birth to by a mother.

You have this built-in problem where your body ages over time.

—

You're too young to remember a time before this present time, but if you buy me a drink I'll tell you. I'll tell you of the lonely human being, back in the days of sweat and myth, the kind of lonely human being who made for himself and for herself a simple machine to have sex with.

Then, over time, yet another machine invented. And then an even better machine, a machine still more and more human.

Then, forward a thousand years, when this new and better machine began to have ideas of its own. This machine graduates to asking for gifts in exchange for love. It is an android now and it asks for money.

It will stand at night with its arms crossed in over lit hallways, for example, not taking off its clothes for you yet, still asking you for money. This kind of thing can only go on for so long before—forward a thousand and then another thousand years—the players eventually switch places.

Now it's the machine who carries the money. Now the machine wears the fashionable suit. Now it's you standing in the hallway with your arms crossed.

This has been a brief history of our present-day android overlords.

—

These androids: they like to walk around. They like to see a human body without its clothes. They like to stare deeply into your bellybutton and consider human mystery.

They are polite and free with their money and they are looking for a good time. (They want to be understood as looking for a good time.)

They tip well when you do something particularly human, like when you laugh or when you have trouble breathing or when you tell a story about your mother.

Don't be so selfish. They just want to learn a little bit about you, what it means to feel, how to pin words to what they feel. But they don't feel anything. That's what they need you for.

And that's what, if you're lucky, they're going to keep needing you for.

WHATEVER A GHOUL'S SUPPOSED TO BE

Shoosh is married with no children and she's older than my mother.

One day she tells me she thinks her husband, Mr. Welch, is a ghoul.

"Out all night," Shoosh says, "skulking around graveyards."

"How do you know?"

"There's an odor," Shoosh says.

—

Shoosh teaches fifth grade and lives in the house across the street from my mother's house.

I used to live in my mother's house. Now I live with Shoosh.

Shoosh had been my teacher at Universal Elementary. She only had to paddle me the one time.

Back then I called her Mrs. Welch.

Now that I'm taller I call her Jane or Shoosh.

(When she was a girl she liked to shush people, etc. And when you're born in a trailer, like she was, sometimes you have to say "shoosh" instead of "shush.")

Shoosh is very thoughtful. She has wide cheekbones and the skeleton of a bird.

Her husband, Mr. Welch, looks like a regular guy, but who can say for certain?

He's a real-estate agent with an office downtown.

Often he'll poke his hairless head into the living room and say, "How're we all doing in here?"

—

The mother's a good enough mother when she isn't full of pills.

How I come to live with Shoosh in the first place is my mother likes to take pills and dance.

When the mother is full of pills, she rattles when she dances.
She likes to dance out in the front yard with the moon as a partner.
She likes to dance in the kitchen with no partner at all.
The yard dances are slow, stately, sad even.
But when she dances in the kitchen, I have to say, it's a little out of control.
She looks like a string puppet. And how, once she gets her legs organized, she's going to come get you.
"This might be difficult for you to hear," the mother once said to me, "but I'm not your mother when I dance."

—

My father moved to California to have a heart attack and start a new family.
My last grandparent died a year ago.
And so then, late one night near the time I've been talking about, I come downstairs to discover what I think is my mother's dead body, there on the long black couch, television tuned to snow, the mother stretched out on her back, mouth open slightly, glass of red wine spilled out in her lap, prescription bottle of pills—one of those jumbo bottles that looks like a miniature trash barrel—tumped over on the coffee table. The name on the label of the bottle isn't my mother's name. The name is the name Jack Danvers. We will never know who Jack Danvers might have been. On the nightstand there are other bottles of other pills with other labels and still other names on the labels, none of the names my mother's name. The mother is wearing nude pantyhose (with a long run up the right leg), black bra, black panties beneath the pantyhose. I can see the shiny laddered c-section scar where they cut her open to pull me out of her all those years of my life ago. The mother now has cigarette ash in her bellybutton and she doesn't seem to be breathing. I take one of the pills from the coffee table and put it in my mouth, scoop up the rest of the pills and palm them into the bottle and put the bottle in my pocket.

I pick up the phone and I call my former teacher and sometimes babysitter Shoosh, whose number is one of the numbers I know.

"No," Shoosh says into the phone, "I'm sure she's still breathing."

"You can't tell from across the street," I say.

"Call 911, sweetheart," Shoosh says. "I'll be right over."

—

So I stay with Shoosh in her little white house while my mother is in treatment.

I sleep in the Welch basement where, Shoosh says, there's not been a silverfish sighting in fifteen years.

I haven't heard anything from Shoosh about ghouls yet, but I will pretty soon.

The basement is just one wide open room with no dividing walls and a washer and dryer tucked beneath the stairs, but Shoosh makes up the idea of a room for me, big yellow rug defining the shape of the space, double bed in a warped wooden frame, a nightstand with an eagle foot lamp, scarred desk for any schoolwork, rectangular tv the husband had previously mounted to the wall back when he'd had plans to make the basement a finished basement, small two-person couch upon which I never sit. For my keep I perform odd chores and sometimes I'm invited to help pick the color of the nail polish Shoosh will wear. Neither do I mind climbing a ladder to clean a gutter or put in a lightbulb. And, if I had my way, I'd always pick the dark blue nail polish for the nails of Shoosh's fingers and toes, but I know Shoosh favors the reds or metallics.

—

We sit on the couch and she holds the wicker nail basket up to me while we watch the big television in the living room. I poke around in the basket, enjoying the heaviness of the small bottles and their shapes and colors. Shoosh likes those tv shows with car crashes and detectives and racy secretaries, which is fine by me. I let my hand hover over one of the blue bottles of polish and then—last second, generous—I pick the silver to make Shoosh happy. She elbows me good naturedly. It's close to bedtime and now we can hear the garage door opening and Mr. Welch's Audi pulling in. After a bit her husband sticks his head into the living room.

"How're we all doing in here?"

Shoosh says, without looking up at him, "Hungry?"

"Nope," he says.

She nods her head like that's the answer she expected.

Mr. Welch heads upstairs, jingling the car keys in his pocket.

After he's gone, Shoosh asks, "Do you smell an odd smell?"

"Not really," I say.

—

One of the things you learn in school is how some of the girls they have in there would like to murder each other.

All of which I report because a girl named Tammy Wellish is the reason Mrs. Welch, back in that fifth-grade class, had to paddle me. The girl Tammy Wellish was a person with a certain darkness, many enemies, blond hair going in three directions and her body constantly radiating the smell of ultralight cigarettes and baked cookies. Tammy was also fond of romance novels and of folding dollar bills into finger rings and of enlisting you to write propaganda about her on the wall in the boys' restroom.

If I had any notoriety as a fifth grader at Universal Elementary it was because I liked comics and I drew fairly well. And Tammy Wellish liked the drawings I passed around about how school was very boring. Therefore she recruited me to draw a takedown of a rich girl named Lynette Arbogast, who was Tammy's nemesis at the time. Thoughtlessly and with a crush I agreed. (Tammy mainly dated middle schoolers but she kept a group of hopefuls around and—it's only now I understand this, not then—I was one of these hopefuls.) I don't remember how Lynette Arbogast ran afoul of Tammy, nor do I remember the girl Lynette all that well, nor does it matter. All I remember is Tammy had me draw Lynette with missing teeth, gramma's underpants falling to her knocked knees, the caption "Portrait of a Slut" beneath. It was the best likeness I could manage, but Tammy wanted to make sure, so she printed out Lynette's name at the top, then tacked the picture to a bulletin board in the hall outside the auditorium. She stood back and looked at it like it was her masterpiece. Only then did I feel bad and worry about possible consequences. The consequences were swift. One of Lynette's friends told Lynette about the drawing, Lynette then of course told Mrs. Welch, which made Mrs. Welch have to send Tammy to the principal, which made Tammy give me up as the artist, which made Mrs. Welch have to paddle me during the lunch hour.

A note from the principal said I was to be served three whacks for my offense.

Shoosh showed me the note.

"I hate this," she said.

I passed the note back to her.

"I'm sorry," I said.

The classroom stood empty and it was just me and Shoosh, stray voices floating from the distant cafeteria like up from a well, the dull rattle of the heat thronging the vents. You remember such details on a day, like this, when you're about to make a friend for life. Of course I didn't think of her as Shoosh yet, not quite yet. Up to this point, to me, she'd just been a teacher, one I liked a little more than I liked other teachers. Now she turned a kid's desk around to face me and she was too tall for the desk and she had to fold down her bird skeleton to get into it. I'd been whacked before and had discovered it wasn't the end of the world, but Shoosh seemed sad and serious about it. Her cheekbones were like blades that had to be pounded into cheekbones and when she was worried or sad, like now, her cheekbones looked like they might cut through her skin. It all made me feel for her, like she was the one in trouble, not me. She'd recently had her dark hair cut very short and you could tell, by the way she kept touching her fingers to her bangs, she wasn't yet comfortable with the haircut. She rested the paddle across her knees and she wouldn't look down at it.

"I'm not a cruel person," she said.

"I know," I said.

She searched my face.

"Then why do I own a paddle?" she said.

"A whack doesn't really hurt that much."

"I don't want you to think I became a teacher," she said, "just so I could paddle children."

"I don't think that."

She pinched the bridge of her nose between her forefinger and thumb.

"I couldn't be about to cry," she said. "That would be ridiculous."

"Okay," I said.

"I hoped I'd make it to summer without having to paddle another one."

"We could lie and say you did," I said.

She nodded.

"And then you'd tell everyone how bad it was?" she said.

"Yes," I said.

"That's good of you," she said, "but I don't want you to have to lie for me."

I nodded. I tried to go another way.

"I deserve it anyway," I said. "I'm guilty. I made the drawing."

"That you're guilty," she said, "doesn't make it right.

I didn't know what to say to that one. We sat looking across small plastic desks at each other. The second hand on the clock above the coat closet kept giving off its drowsy thunk.

"You've been very kind," she said, "and you really didn't have to be."

"It's all right, Mrs. Welch."

"Okay," she said.

"Okay," I said.

She stood with the paddle and I stood and leaned over the desk with my palms flat on the desktop. She walked around behind, put her hand on the small of my back, lining up the target.

"Every time I do this," she said, "I have terrible dreams."

—

Three whacks and three years later I stand in the Welch yard policing crabgrass with Mrs. Jane Welch, who is Shoosh. She still has the same short haircut, like a boy. We are now closer to the same height. Across the road is the small white empty house that is my mother's house. My mother is in treatment for another couple of weeks. I want her to come back, to be okay, but I don't want to leave Shoosh's. I want my mother to be alive and happy, to go on, in some ways, without me, or without having to worry about me, the shy vulnerable fact of that c-section scar, yes, and the truth that, back when she had me, my mother was only four years older than I am now. Summer, Sunday, Shoosh's husband in the living room watching baseball loud enough I can follow the game outside in the yard. Shoosh wears clamdiggers and bright yellow flip-flops that look like they're made of banana candy. Her toenails are silver. She's wearing a baseball hat and a pair of black gloves she tells me she's pulled from the lost-and-found at Universal Elementary. The hat is a hat she always wears when working in the yard and it's blue and for some reason it says, in all caps across the front panel, the word "LUNCHEONETTE." I stand in the yard on one side of the front walk and Shoosh stands in the yard on the other side of the front walk. And on that front walk, between us, is a little stack of ceramic dessert plates and a spray bottle filled with white vinegar. I have a dessert plate in my hand and so does Shoosh. She's taught me how to look for tillers of crabgrass and she's taught me the word "tillers" and I'm told I'm a big help because I have younger eyes. I am also high on one and a half of Jack Danvers's pills and the lateness of the afternoon is heavy across the neighborhood and the cicadas just now kick on, like someone flipped a switch. I'm so focused on what I'm doing that the sound makes me jump. And now I think I see a tiller and I put my foot near it, call Shoosh over to get her official word. She picks up the spray bottle and comes over to me and she kneels on the grass.

"Got you," she says.

She sprays a cloud of vinegar and I bend down and cover the tiller with an upturned plate. The pills of the man Jack Danvers—whoever he might have been—make you thoughtful and slow and you can see the tiny bugs moving down beneath the root matting of the grasses, the roots under there pale at first and then going a burnt ruby-red almost like a living network and making the lawn a single thing. Shoosh raises up and puts her hand on my shoulder and we both look down at the upturned white plate. It looks like a tiny alien landing marker. To any passerby, we'd seem a strange pair, the two of us—not exactly mother and son, but with more or less the same haircut—gazing down with a sense of accomplishment at a dessert plate overturned in the grass and acting like it belongs there. Shoosh smells like light sweat and soap and water and I've started having dreams where, wherever I am in the dream, Shoosh comes to pick me up in a horse-drawn carriage. In the flip-flops her feet are pale and dirty and I imagine biting into the yellow candy of her left flip-flop and it pulling away from my mouth in strands like taffy. Now Shoosh frees this same left foot from the flip-flop and touches her big toe to the dessert plate.

"Let's kill a few more tillers," she says.

—

We sit on the steps of the front porch looking out at the yard, the four or five dessert plates flipped over here and there in no obvious pattern, dusk, lightning bugs doing that slow dipping flight that makes them look overloaded with themselves. Shoosh is talking about her husband, who is now watching the news in the house behind us.

"Out driving all night," Shoosh says, nodding. "Out visiting graveyards."

"How do you know?"

"There's an odor," she says.

"Like what?"

"A light one," she says, "like when you turn over a log. A worse one where you think something's dead."

"Sometimes you hear about zombies," I say.

"Ghouls are alive and eat the dead. That's one difference," she says. She glances over at me to see how I'm taking such information.

"I worry about telling you all this," she says.

"It's okay."

We sit there for a bit. It's one of those confused evenings when the moon and the sun are up at the same time.

"Also," she says, changing the subject, looking off to not embarrass me, "you ought not take those pills like you do."

"I know it," I say.

"But how bad are they?"

"Pretty bad," I say.

I have the bottle in my pocket and I show it to Shoosh.

"Who's Jack Danvers?" she asks.

"He's whoever mom's dealer stole the pills from."

Shoosh nods and opens the bottle and pulls out the wadded tissue and looks in and pokes her finger around.

"I'll sample this little old half of one maybe," Shoosh says.

She plucks the half pill from the bottle. I know the other half of this same pill is in my stomach already. Shoosh pops her half in her mouth and swallows it.

"Anxieties," she says.

"For sure," I say.

"I feel like I should say a little prayer or something," she says.

She hands me the bottle and we sit staring out at the upturned plates, watching cars pass, watching the moon replace the sun.

"Another difference is," she says, "is ghouls look just like people. They talk and reason and pretend to have ideas. It's tough to know it when you're standing in front of one."

"How do you know it?"

"The smell," she says, "but not everyone is sensitive. Also, they don't like to look you in the eye. And you never see them eat."

"I wonder if I know anyone that way," I say.

"Probably you do," she says.

She glances over again.

"Don't tell anyone I talk to you about these things," she says. "People don't want to understand what's in front of them."

"I wouldn't say anything."

Shoosh bumps me with her elbow.

"I didn't think you would."

—

Somebody down the street, this way or that, or maybe in the alley back of us, lets off a string of firecrackers. In not too long you can smell the gunpowder drifting in on the small breeze. Sitting on a porch next to someone like Shoosh, when you've done a fine day's work—and how she treats you like a better person than you think you are and doesn't take your pills away, and even if she does scare you a little when she tells you facts about ghouls—it all makes the world seem narrower, slower, less all over the place.

She waves her hand in front of her face.

"It feels," she says of the pill, "like Time is getting curious about me."

I hold up my hand in front of my face like Shoosh.

"I hadn't thought of it that way."

—

Some nights when the Welches are asleep I sneak out of their little house and cross the street and key back into my mother's house and walk around, looking into closets, straightening up, poking through my chest of drawers for the odd forgotten t-shirt I'll suddenly decide I can no longer live without. It's partly because, even though I don't want to live there anymore, I miss my old room. It's partly because I can steal some of Mom's cigarettes and search the cabinets and couch cushions for more loose pills. It's partly because, as familiar as the house is, it now feels strange and past tense, like one of those houses a famous person lived in and they roped it off, after, into a museum.

But a lot of it is simply because I feel bad having to masturbate in the Welch basement. It feels ungrateful, impolite, nor do I want to have wet dreams over there either and be the pervert who has to worry about how to hide the sheets in the laundry. This would be so embarrassing for all of us. And it's worse when sometimes images of Shoosh—when I don't want them to, and no matter how hard I try to keep it from happening—pop into my head during, which when it happens it feels more than impolite, to think of her like that, under her own roof, maybe closer to betrayal. I know since I'm a boy Shoosh doesn't think of me that way and, in truth, I don't think that way about Shoosh either, not really. It's just I think she's kind and she smells nice and she trusts me with things she doesn't say to other people. So I think about her holding me and asking me to look at her face, those things people do and say when they're alone and without the business of their clothes. And it's easier to think such thoughts when I'm safely across the street from where her body is. And I'll look at Shoosh's house out the window of my bedroom and I'll imagine her inside that house, breathing behind a closed door, kicking her covers off because she's too hot.

All of which is what I'm doing that next night, sitting on my bed in the mother's house with my shorts pulled down, looking out my bedroom window at my former teacher Shoosh's dark house, around two in the morning or so. And I'm at it that way for a while until I feel the adrenaline in my chest, feel it even before I know what I'm seeing, which is that there's a man standing in the Welch side yard, hidden by the shadows of the trees, yet lit, a little, by the streetlights of the alley. The alley light comes through the trees green, washes into the man standing there half in the dark, gives his skin a greenish cast. Turns out I'm not the only one watching the Welch house. I pull up my shorts and move to the window and look more closely. By the shine of the alley light on the man's head, now, I can tell it's Mr. Welch himself, which should make the situation less troubling, but it doesn't. It doesn't because he's just standing there with his hands limp at his sides, it doesn't because he's swaying a little and his shoulders shake like it sometimes happens when you're crying, it doesn't because Shoosh has told me she thinks her husband isn't her husband anymore. He stands that way a long time, too long a time, without moving. He's far away and there's no way he can see me, but when he turns his head in my direction, like he's felt my eyes on him, I drop to the floor and hide.

—

I don't go visit my mother in the treatment center. And when she's released, I don't go with Shoosh to pick her up. And when Shoosh comes into the house and tells me my mother is back home, I don't go across the street to see her right away, not for a few minutes. I sit at the kitchen table in the Welch house, looking out the window and across the street. My mother is out there, has come out there, is sitting on the steps of the front porch of her house, smoking a cigarette, elbow up on her knee, resting her chin in the cup of her hand. She won't look over at the Welch house. She's wearing cut-offs and a former red t-shirt of mine that says "Universal Warriors" on it. She's gained a little weight and she somehow seems even younger than she did before. I look so much like her I think I only see her, like now, whenever I'm really looking. I stand up from the table and I go out the Welch front door and down the walk to the curb. I look over at her with the sun high between us and she looks over at me.

"Now you're all wary of me," she says.

I turn my head down the street this way and the other, like to see if a car's coming.

"You're not dead," I say.

"You wouldn't know it by how I feel," she says.

I don't say anything. She's got her smokes next to her and she flips the lid and takes one out and lights it. She holds the pack up so I can see it and she raises her eyebrows. I walk across the street and up the walk and I take a cigarette and sit down next to her.

"House looks good," she says.

"I cleaned a little," I say.

She lights the cigarette for me and her toes grip the wooden step of the porch.

"Shoosh says you're thinking about staying at hers a little longer," she says.

"I could have told you."

"I think she wanted to make it easy on us."

"Probably."

"Shoosh feeling okay?"

"What do you mean?" I ask.

"She looked a little," Mom says, "I don't know." She makes a spider movement with her hand. "Pale, I guess."

"I hadn't noticed," I say.

"And it's okay by me anyways," Mom says.

"That she looks pale?"

"If you stay with her a while."

"Okay."

Her cigarette is running lopsided and she points the cherry at herself, blows on it to even it up.

"Didn't want you to feel bad about it."

"Thank you."

"Don't you forget I'm over here, though."

"I won't."

She nods.

"Sorry about it," she says in general.

"It's okay," I say.

"I didn't mean for it to be my fault," she says, "but it was."

—

I don't think the Welches are home and I get a glass of water from the kitchen sink and I make a ham sandwich and I sit at the Welch kitchen table, eating the sandwich and looking at a WWII comic about a tank crew haunted by the ghost of a Civil War general. I don't know how long I'm sitting there until I feel a little scampering feeling in my chest and I turn around and Mr. Welch is standing in the doorway to the living room, looking at me.

"Hello," I say.

"Hello," he says.

"I was just getting a sandwich."

I show him the sandwich.

He stands there for a bit, takes off his glasses and wipes the lenses with his shirt.

"I just wanted to say," he says finally, "how happy we are to have you here."

—

Some nights and late, when Mr. Welch isn't at home, Shoosh will take me out driving around Universal, looking for Mr. Welch's Audi, looking for signs of him.

Shoosh's car is a tiny Omni hatchback and it feels, usually in a good way, like riding around in a bumper car.

She'll drive through downtown Universal and off Main and past Mr. Welch's real-estate offices, which are housed in what I believe used to be an old Burger Chef. Shoosh will drive back and forth down the street, looking for her husband's car, then she'll flip around and drive down the alley, looking at the parking lot behind the office. His car won't be there either. Then she'll drive us to the east, to Parker Haven Cemetery, where she thinks her husband, the ghoul, might go. He won't be there either. Then she'll drive us west and a little south to the other big cemetery, Common Grove, drive us around the loops, the switchbacks, through one parking lot, through the other parking lot. He won't be there and he won't be there.

—

"Well," she says one night, "I've got an idea."

We're at Common Grove and no sightings of Mr. Welch.

"What's your idea," I ask her.

"Patience," she says.

She drives us out of the cemetery loop and gets back on the highway and she takes us south toward the Kentucky border.

I haven't told Shoosh about the night I saw her husband, in the wee hours, out in the yard, staring back at his own house. I haven't told her because I'd have to explain what I was doing over at my mother's house in the first place, but mainly because I'm not sure if the information would make her feel better or worse about her husband. We've got frozen drinks from DQ, mine blue, Shoosh's red. It's a good time, driving around with Shoosh, smelling her soap-and-water smell, a good time marred only slightly by the fact that we're out looking for ghouls, which probably don't exist. School seems far away and Shoosh sings along with a Linda Ronstadt song off classic radio and her voice isn't too bad. She tells me how, when she was a girl, she used to pray she'd grow up to look like Linda Ronstadt.

"Round bottom," Shoosh says, "little push-up nose."

"I don't know if I know what she looks like," I say.

"How dare you?" Shoosh says.

—

"Do you remember when I took you to the zoo?" Shoosh asks.

I look over at her. The speedometer is tilting pretty high into its range, but it's hard to say from the passenger seat. I have the pills of Jack Danvers with me and Shoosh and I are as curious about Time as Time is curious about us. It's past midnight and we're across the border into Kentucky now. Despite the frozen drink my mouth is dry and the green lights of the dashboard light up Shoosh's face in little floating triangles.

"I don't think I remember a zoo," I say.

"This was well before you were even in my class," she says.

"I didn't know I knew you that far back," I say.

"You did," she says. "You wouldn't have been making memories then. This was right when your mom and dad moved into that house. It was the zoo up in Indianapolis we went to," she says. "I can't remember why your mom wanted me to watch you. Maybe she and your father were going to the slots in Tunica, which they sometimes did, didn't they?" She paused and she didn't seem sure if my parents went to Tunica or not. She said, "You and I were both so excited to see the animals, but when we got there they made us sad. The cages were small. It was very hot. The animals weren't happy."

"Yes," I say, "I think I remember."

I don't really remember. But I'm not lying either. As Shoosh tells the story I can feel a little pulse of feeling I can't put words or pictures to, a feeling like a sadness I'm familiar with.

"You wanted me to see if they'd turn the bears loose from their cages," she says. "They were in pretty rough shape. They had big hunks of dead hair falling off them. I knew you were a pretty good kid, even back then."

I watch the kudzu flying past in the dark. She rattles the Omni off the highway and down a gravel road where the only lighting is her headlights. I have this silly vision of Shoosh driving me out into the woods and murdering me in some ditch because she knows, even though I don't, that I'm a ghoul. The sky is shallow above and black forever. We pass a sign on the road that says we're headed toward a cemetery called Evergreen Cemetery. Shoosh tells me this is the cemetery where her husband's parents and his sister are buried and it might be the cemetery her husband would think to prowl.

"And I still can't half believe," she says through the triangles on her face, "that I married a man from Kentucky."

—

Evergreen's a small cemetery on a slight rise and there's a parking lot at the base and Shoosh pulls in and parks the Omni. Gravel dust follows us in from the road and the engine ticks annoyedly and there aren't any other cars around.

Mr. Welch isn't here, either.

"I don't know his first name," I say.

"Henry," Shoosh says.

"Henry," I say.

"Maybe," Shoosh says, "Henry just parks somewhere and walks around all night."

"Or maybe it's nothing," I say.

I worry about saying this but it seems to go over okay.

"If it's nothing," she says gently, "then why isn't he at the office?"

"Maybe it's something we haven't thought about," I say.

"A woman?"

"Or whatever," I say.

"I've thought about that," she says. "And wouldn't that be nice? And wouldn't that," she says, "be so much better?"

—

One night or the next night I wake from a dream where I'm on a sinking cruise ship and Shoosh pulls up in a horse-drawn carriage and tosses me a life preserver and drives me back to the safety of her castle. It's the middle of the night in the Welch basement and the dream is obvious and I'm not alone. I sit up and look down the bed and it's Shoosh herself, sitting on the little two-person couch, in a white robe, in the more or less dark. She's wearing her LUNCHEONETTE baseball hat, which does not go with the robe, and she's looking at me.

"You scared me," I say.

"I'd hate it if I woke you up."

"A dream did it," I say.

"Dreams can be confusing."

"Yes."

"I dream a lot of times," she says, "of just regular, boring things, like going to the doctor, or like going shopping for groceries, which doesn't sound that bad," she says, her voice flat, seeming to run on without her, "except," she says, "when you wake up, you can't remember if you actually went to the doctor or bought groceries or not, you can't remember if it's real or not, and sooner or later," she says, "you can't tell the difference between what you dreamed you did and what you've actually done."

"I have these ones," I say, "where you pick me up in a carriage and take me places."

"I'm glad I'm helpful in them," she says.

"You are," I say.

She smiles and she realizes she's wearing the baseball hat and it surprises her. She takes off the hat and puts it on the cushion next to her. I keep the covers on me and push myself to the foot of the bed and I sit there, legs crossed. Shoosh keeps pulling her robe more and more tightly closed around her. Her cheeks are flushed in a way they usually aren't and she holds her mouth in a strange, stiff way I haven't seen before, like she's put her face muscles up on stilts. The cheekbones cut into the skin of her cheeks. We hear the distant sound of the second-floor toilet flushing, her husband moving around up there, some creaking of the floorboards. Shoosh looks up at the basement ceiling.

"I don't want him to know I'm down here," she says. "I don't want him to find me."

"We'll be quiet," I say.

"We'll be quiet," she says.

"Are you okay?"

"Do I smell bad?" she asks. "Is it me?"

"No," I say.

"You can't tell it from there," she says.

She stands up from the couch and steps closer to me so I can smell her.

"Like soap and water," I say.

She sits back down.

"And you're not just," she says, "sitting there lying to me?"

"I wouldn't."

"Because what if Henry smells the way he does," she says, "because he sleeps next to me. What if I've got it all backwards," she says, "and he's not the evil one?"

—

My mother is sitting on the long black couch in the living room, the couch where I found her, not too long ago, in pantyhose and with cigarette ash in her bellybutton. I'm standing at the hall window, looking across the street at the Welch house. I'm wearing Shoosh's LUNCHEONETTE baseball hat. There's an ambulance parked out in front of the Welch house and a black sedan, parked behind it, with the words "Mobile Crisis" on the side. Shoosh's husband, Henry, is standing on the lawn with his arms crossed, talking to a man with a clipboard. Shoosh will go in for a seventy-two-hour hold, or for as long as the insurance lasts.

"Why 'Luncheonette'?" the mother asks.

"I'm not sure either," I say.

She nods and puts her feet up on the coffee table.

"Your dad and I used to go to Tunica," she says. "That's true. Why he took me, I don't know. He didn't like to gamble, and he didn't like live music, and he didn't like to party, and he didn't like going to restaurants, and he didn't like to stay up late. God knows why either one of us married the other."

She lights a cigarette and bulges her lighter between the box of smokes and the cellophane cover that covers it. I turn around and look back out the window.

"But," the mother says, "I don't think Shoosh ever took you to a zoo."

"She seemed really certain about it," I say. "I felt like I even remembered it a little."

"What do you remember?"

"Nothing we did," I say, "just, when she was talking about it, I felt a sad feeling."

My mother picks up the remote control for the tv and points it.

"That kind of feeling," she says, trailing off.

"Yeah?"

"Yeah," she agrees, "that kind of feeling could really come from anywhere."

—

On cable we're watching one of the *Friday the 13th* movies, Mom and I, I don't remember which one. I've popped some popcorn in the air popper and put it in a bowl and put the bowl between us on the long black couch. The mother likes a little garlic salt on her popcorn. I don't, though neither do I really mind it. My objection to garlic salt is part of a little script the mother likes to run, where she's the wild card and I'm the square. She waggles her eyebrows and gets up from the couch and goes to the kitchen for the garlic salt and she comes back and sits down cross-legged.

"God help us," I say.

"I'll just sprinkle a little on my side," she says, winking.

"It's a bowl. There aren't sides."

"Garlic is good for the spirit," she says.

"That sounds made up," I say.

"It's all made up," she says.

She hides her eyes and the killer Jason is wearing a flour sack over his head.

"I thought he wore a fucking hockey mask," she says.

"I think he gets the hockey mask in the next one."

One thing I notice about the killer, Jason, though, is how gentle he is. Not the killer, not the character Jason, but I mean whoever the actor is. He's a big guy and you can tell he knows how big he is. He's careful with his fellow cast members. In one scene he seems to allow an actress to bring her throat to his hand instead of the other way around. In another scene, where he's swinging a machete at a different actress, you can tell he's being thoughtful about the arc of the swing, keeping it short and close to his own body. In a later scene, wrestling with a young male actor, he looks to hold himself up on his elbows instead of bearing down. I miss Shoosh and Shoosh doesn't want anyone visiting her in the mental health facility. If they get her meds straightened out, she'll be home in a matter of days. The facility isn't really a facility, her husband Henry has told me, so much as it's just a wing in the hospital. I'd been picturing some kind of asylum from the old days, bars in the windows. And I'd like to go see her, but I think, if I were in her place, I wouldn't want visitors either. And meanwhile, sometimes, late at night when I'm in my room, in my bed, I can hear the mother, my mother, dancing, softly, secretly, in her bedroom, which means she's taking pills again. She's taking them behind closed doors. She's got a job now at the CBS plant and seems to be doing well, but through our shared wall, each night, I can hear the tinny blare of the headphones she wears, the swish of her feet on the wooden floor. She's not dancing in the kitchen yet, nor in the yard and out in the open, but I know it's coming. Now I look over at her on the couch and she seems alive, this mother, present enough, real enough. She lights a cigarette and picks at a hangnail on her toe. On screen the actor beneath the potato sack is using a spear to murder a blond girl who has fallen to the ground. Jason extends the spear so slowly that, instead of killing her with it, it looks like he wants her to grab onto it. And then, you know, once she grabs onto it, he'll use it to help pull her up.

—

That night I walk to the Phillips station to get some cigarettes for the mother and to rent another horror from the small wall of movies they've got over there. Coming out the door of the house, I notice, across the street, there's a white LeBaron in the Welch driveway. It's a car I've not seen before, but I don't pay it any mind. I walk down the one block and over the next and walk a slant across the fairgrounds and over toward the highway. The interior of the Phillips is cold from the air conditioning and I shuffle the aisles blankly and poke at individually wrapped pastries while I let the sweat dry off. The movies are in the back corner, between a drink case and a pyramid of motor oil. I'm trying to decide between a modern-day Frankenstein movie and another *Friday the 13th* when I look over and see the girl Tammy Wellish, my fifth-grade crush. She's thinner and I don't remember her hair being that color and she's holding hands with a dark-headed man who looks like he could be thirty years old.

"I thought that was you," she says.

She hugs me to her and she smells like baby powder and lotion.

"I thought you moved away," I say.

"Moved away," she says, squinting one eye, "then moved back. I'll go to Madison in the fall."

"I go to Madison," I say.

"Charlie," Tammy says to the dark-headed man. She points at me. "This here's one of my former soldiers."

—

We talk in the aisles and I find out Tammy's family bought a house in my mother's neighborhood. I'd forgotten the funny, sweet way she talks, where some of the Ls turn into Ws. We tell each other we've gotten tall and she asks me if I still draw comics and she invites me to a cookout her family's doing in the park for July 4th. The boyfriend Charlie, I can tell, doesn't want me at any cookout. They rent a comedy with a robot in it and we say goodbye and they head out hand in hand and they get into an El Camino in the slow motion of the heat. I rent the *Friday the 13th* and the clerk is a man who knows my mother and doesn't mind selling me cigarettes even though I'm underage. I get a soda and I drink it walking across the fairgrounds and chuck the empty bottle in a ditch. I worry I may have rented the exact same *Friday the 13th* movie the mother and I just watched on cable. From the hug Tammy gave me, my t-shirt smells like baby powder and lotion. I exit the fairgrounds and walk the block over and then the block back and up. And going up my mother's street I see, in the Welch driveway, that same white LeBaron, except this time with a tallish blond woman standing beside it, keys in her hand.

—

The LeBaron is gone next morning and it's gone most of the next day. It's back again that night. Henry Welch has a girlfriend. Not so surprising, really. The blond woman I saw the night before, standing next to the LeBaron, is, was, a woman taller than Shoosh, though maybe not all that much younger, not more beautiful, not less beautiful. For no reason (though it will turn out, later, that I'm right) I imagine the blond woman being Henry's secretary down at the real-estate offices. I sit on the edge of my bed, looking out the window at the Welch house, the white LeBaron in the drive. Shoosh will come home, soon, with meds adjusted. She'll tell me how we'll need, going forward, to look out for each other. Soon my mother will have to return to treatment. Soon I'll live in the Welch basement again. Through the shared bedroom wall I can hear the tinny sound of my mother's headphones, the swish of her feet on the wooden floor.

I think back to that night I saw Henry Welch standing in his side yard, staring at his own house. For what reason? Out of guilt? Out of fear of the darkness working through his wife's mind? For the same fear of night and the unknown I'm feeling right now? It really doesn't matter. It's quiet in the next room, which means the pills have put the mother to sleep. Ready now, I stand from the bed and I find Shoosh's baseball hat and I put it on. I walk from my room into the kitchen and get a steak knife from the silverware drawer. Tomorrow, even though Shoosh doesn't want visitors, I'll go to the hospital. I'll visit Shoosh and let her be mad at me if she wants. I'll tell her all about what I've done, what I'm about ready to do, what I'm already in the middle of doing. I go out the back door—which is quieter than the front door—and out into the calm hot night. I walk around the house to the front, cross the street, walk up the Welch driveway. The Welch house is dark and quiet. I kneel at the rear tire of the blond woman's LeBaron, take Shoosh's hat off my head, hold it against the tire, drive the knife through the hat and into the tire. The tire coughs and flattens and the car sinks a little, like it's disappointed. I stand up and look down. The knife pins Shoosh's baseball hat to the tire, like a message saying *no thank you*, a message from the universe of Shoosh. People are small and fragile and they try to protect you. Love burns its way into the body of a ghoul. It's night and the moon, reflected in the blade of the knife, can be counted on to keep its mouth shut. I feel wrong for what I've done here, Henry, wrong and also perfect.

AFTERNOON WITH SUPERNATURAL ORPHAN

Near the melon bin of the supermarket called Kreitler's, in the heart of the American Midwest, summer of the 2,026 year since the birth of the supposed Christ, I'm questioned by a balding sack of a man who thinks I'm lost. "Where's your mother?" says he, the store manager, leaning down to look into my eyes. His name tag says Brandon Walters. I reach up and touch his cheek with my tiny hand. Gently I talk to him in a language mostly demons and witches have used. I talk right through the center of his forehead. What is the name of this language? There is no name for this language since, without a name, it will never die. Nor do I have a name either. The demons didn't think it fair to give me one; the witches bide their time. The smile drops from the face of Brandon Walters and his eyes cloud and he straightens, unpins the nametag from his shirt pocket, lets it clatter to the tile. He isn't a man named Brandon Walters anymore. He manages nothing but breathing. He stands there, swaying longingly, like he wants to become a tree.

—

I see the family I want. I watch the family I want. I don't know why I want them. It's a feeling in the chest, like a pocket of cold water lurking underneath the warm. The family: they move through their own sad weather, look you, lit by the red shine of packaged meat. They are strangers to me, this family, but I know them. They're handsome and young. The mother, Carol, real estate, a halo of amber flecking around her head, six angels riding in her right eyetooth. The father, John, unemployed musician, consumer of Valtrex. Two children, the youngest a little boy about my size, hair the color of cooked salmon, very into *Star Wars*; the daughter older, hugless and unbeknownst, peering down into the well of her phone, blond.

—

Now they come down the bread aisle, in loose formation around the selected cart, the little boy arguing white over wheat, pulling at his father's sleeve. The father wears the tattoo of a bygone cartoon bird on his forearm and the mother, Carol, looks off down the aisle toward the yogurt case, like whatever she's been dreaming of at night might be stored there. The Mayflower family. What their energy is at home, they tote it along, they spread it around in public microbes. I can smell the bright soup smell of the Mayflower kitchen, feel the cramped circus of the bedtime. I feel how everyone in the unit is tired of the boy, his lurid optimism, his embrace of the funbreads, even his name, which is Chip. And to this son, but perhaps to everyone who is alive in the world, the father says, "All right already," tosses the poison bread into the cart, Carol's eyes hole-punching the back of her husband's head, the daughter sighing off, feigning an interest in the bagel, hoping herself a cut above the going DNA.

—

For some reason the daughter's name does not come to me, a bit of a blank, this girl, an untold concern. Laura? Lauren? I look away from the daughter, back to Carol the mother, the mother who has just now seen me, her angel-tooth shining, eyes pausing, noting, moving on. I'm standing small in famous short pants near the grape jelly, looking washable and forlorn. Angels, like demons, have nothing between their ears or legs. I say to myself, and to the mother, Carol with the halo, Carol, I say, you are the one.

—

It's hard to know if I'm a girl or a boy. I toddle up to Carol and I take her hand. She looks down to see what it is that might have ahold of her. She sees what she sees, a child somewhat thin and needing touch and care, perhaps her own baby. I give her time, the time she needs. She sees me, she sees her own child. I say up to her, in English, "Mother, can we go to the botanical gardens later?"

—

My tone is educated, formal. I seem a well-mannered child. And this is no accident: Carol the mother *loves* the thing known as the botanical gardens. She'd like to picnic there, small frenched sandwiches and a dessert of berries, but she's found herself marooned in a no-picnic family. There are many families like that, Carol, don't blame yourself. They run on cheap fuel. They look to clocks for love. Carol's eyes go white and she lifts me into the baby seat of the cart, feeling the ease of my weight, feeling to herself how she has felt my weight many times before, even within her body, which she hasn't. "Of course we can, baby," she says, slightly confused that she doesn't know a name to call me, and the other Mayflowers hear her voice, the affection in her tone when she speaks. They turn to look at me in my silver seat before the mother, my legs a dangle, then they look at the mother, the mother who tousles my hair. And I am already the favorite. I smile forcefully at them, these three who are not the mother, one by one, husband to daughter to boy, my eyes saying, "Too late," saying, "Death is a promise made to no one." And they feel this truth in their teeth, they go back to doing what they were doing, with no question. I don't even have to make them be a tree. Sometimes it's too easy, Carol, it's too easy for us, for we are in love. I can keep you alive forever. I believe your daughter's name, this sister's name, is Lana? Tell me, Mother, about *your* mother, about your memories of girlhood, about your infidelities, planned and unplanned. I once sat on the knee of a king who bought me with my weight in treasure. Joan of Arc taught me how to pick the right skipping stone. Mother, you can name me whenever you're ready to name me. I can be patient. I'm thousands of years old.

THE GODS IN SMALL DOSES

My mother told King Theseus how my cousin Angela was more than just another peasant girl with a big dick and a head full of wedding songs.

My mother told the king how there was danger in such a girl, one who could communicate with vegetable life, one with spider blood in her veins.

I called Angela "Double A" because her middle name also began with an A.

I called Angela "Double A" because she didn't like the name Angela.

—

This was that bad year Double A's pythoness mother was strangled to death, in the Temple of Zeus, for seeing the wrong future.

My mother didn't want the orphan Double A coming to live with us, as such a girl would have a bad influence upon her son, her son being me.

Hence the testimony, hence King Theseus.

I didn't witness this testimony, only heard it, second hand, from this girl I knew who did the king's toes. It went like this: the king listened to my mother, the king broke for lunch, the king returned, napkin tucked forgotten in his shirt collar. Then with his gavel he sent the girl Double A, as novice, to the House of Pasiphae, down near the harbor of Athens, where the port widows would teach her to read a book while sitting in a nice chair and to hug a man correctly and they might even show her what a bathtub was. Not such a bad deal if you thought about it, not such a bad deal if you didn't own a bathtub, which we didn't.

Nor did it *necessarily* mean, my mother said later, that Double A would be a prostitute, or at least not forever. Those port widows knew how develop a mystery, etc., tall boots, frill frill, take care of the money, much wisdom. Double A was no virgin either (I'm not saying anything you don't already know) and she'd been born a boy into this world on a day when the moon overstayed till afternoon and an owl was seen working an abacus with its beak down near the Sacred Gate. These days Double A shaved her legs with a seashell and she whispered secrets to Hecate and Attis when she should have turned her heart to sweetness and sent her prayers directly to the brainchild Athena.

—

So I guess it was the king's thinking that the wiles of Pasiphae would not be likely to horrify such a girl.

Double A wore white dresses of her own design, dresses that seemed always in the flow of motion, even on those days when the ship sails of the harbor drooped breathless.

Her father had been my mother's older brother (this brother, my uncle, gored by a boar in his own pear orchard back when Double A was young) and it was said she possessed her Delphic mother's visionary gift and might be able to read your thoughts.

By the time she was fifteen, which was right now, everyone was afraid of her.

With her two parents dead and an infant brother and sister gone directly from the womb to Hades (to my two little undead cousins: may you cruise freely in the underloam and never hunger for the bean), Double A, with her invented dresses and freeform dark hair, was said to fly broomsticks with death. The taint was on her. And also she was tall and lovely, like a bird walking the shoreline of the future. Not out of the realm of possibility that a god or goddess might slide down the big hill and play rapture with her. Or maybe jealous Hera would be moved to take on an unassuming shape, gift Double A with a poisoned undergarment. You just never knew. In Athens, where you didn't want to be too pretty, Double A was too pretty, a lure, a disturbance.

—

I wasn't good-looking by any means. I wasn't that smart. I loved my mother and I didn't like to go against her, but I knew Double A wasn't trash.

The first time Double A made an impression on me, back when we were much younger, she'd held my hand when I was scared during a meteor shower. She was only a year older and I was a boy. But she seemed all grown up, took it upon herself to look out for me. This was in a family backyard somewhere where we had gathered to picnic and witness the celestial portent. Double A squeezed my hand and winked at me as the stars fell. I knew from her gentle presence how I would not be harmed by the universe. And when I brought back my hand, she'd pressed into it—like the gift of a secret jewel—a little piece of pomegranate candy, wrapped in a wrapper and everything.

—

The mud house I lived in with my mother stood nearish to the port. That summer after Double A's sentencing, she'd sometimes sneak from the House of Pasiphae to visit me. The guard dogs refused to bark at her and at least two security guards wanted her to love them and to therefore stop moving around so much. So she'd promise both dog and guard she'd be back before dawn and she'd run through the children's cemetery and up the long hill to my street. She'd duck into an alley whenever the citizen watch passed by, smoking their cigarettes and talking about the wrestling matches. And then she'd come breathing in through my window, feet cold and wet from the dew, hide her head under the covers so the gods would be less likely see her hair, but you could still feel the sonics coming off her heart, like a signal. The sonics were family love and I knew this because they vibrated in my heart, too. Probably love matters less in the clouds because of how a god lasts forever, or why else did they keep sliding down from the mount, turning all the sub-virgins into stars? Double A had a face long like a plains animal, so dark-headed her hair brought about bedtime and made the night bugs confused. She'd be breathless in the white dress and under the blanket we'd say hello and talk with each other. I'd tell her how I wanted to be a writer of plays like those I'd sometimes watched performed down in the public theater by the sea. Or I'd tell her how I regretted not being born good-looking enough, to the point where I might not have a future because my mother couldn't get any landed local men to mentor me. Double A would tell me how in Athens the word "mentor" maybe didn't mean what I thought it did. She wasn't my older cousin for nothing. Yes, she'd admit I wasn't much to look at, but she'd add that some girls cherished different things in a boy, things other than looks, things like sweetness and calmness and devotion and how, anyway, I reminded her of her father, my mother's dead brother and my dead uncle, who had been an ugly and most lovable man. Then she'd tell me what she'd learned, with her new port education, of the Cretan witch Pasiphae, tales of terror that I loved and I hated to hear. And we'd whisper so my mother wouldn't know that we lay together. And we'd lie together side by side and sometimes Double A would press her ear against my ear so she could hear my thoughts.

—

"So then Pasiphae's husband—the king—ejaculated actual scorpions into the body of his mistress."

This was one night, near the time I've been talking about, Double A in my room, having escaped the port widows. There was a little smoked ice chip of moon in the sky. The mud-walled room smelled like mud. Double A smelled like sea salt and limes. I'd nearly fallen asleep at the beginning of her Pasiphae story, but the ending woke me up.

"Who could come up with something like that?"

"Centipedes too."

"No more, please," I said.

"It's definitely worse for the mistress," Double A said, "but I wouldn't want to be the king, either."

"Wait," I said, "does 'ejaculate' mean what I think it means?"

"I'm afraid it does," she said.

I didn't say anything. She elbowed me.

"I can tell you're worried," she said, "but I have no plans to hex you."

"I trust you," I said.

She lifted her empty palm like she was holding something balanced on it.

"Do you want to see my invisible centipede?" she asked.

I told her to knock it off and we lay there for a while under the covers. I looked down at her bare feet. She did a little puppet show with her big toes, where one toe was in love with the other toe and the other toe kept running away.

—

Then I fell asleep and woke up and she was looking at me.

"I like it that you fall asleep," she said. "It means you're not afraid of me."

"Who says I'm not afraid of you?"

"You're afraid in the right way," she said. She rolled over on her back. She said, "Let me press my ear against yours so I can hear your thoughts."

I rolled over on my back so we could get our ears lined up right. I didn't want to harbor, nor for Double A to think I might be harboring. It was important to me to have my mind opened, to make my thoughts readable. I lay there very calmly so she might hear all of what was in my head, even the things, maybe, I didn't even know about.

"You're thinking you miss me when I'm not around," she said, "and also you're thinking," she said, "about how you're afraid of death."

"You're never wrong," I said.

She said, "You like to watch an animal drink water from a stream and you wish your mother would let you own a dog."

"This is really incredible," I said.

"Try listening to my thoughts," she said.

I wasn't gifted like she was. I pressed my ear into her ear as hard as I could.

"I can't hear anything," I said.

She put her face over my face and kissed me.

"You're better off," she said. "There's some weird stuff going on in there."

—

You'll recall in Athena's namesake city that year we were finding albino salt eels breeding in knots in the wells and the cisterns. Then a brackish swamp seeped in overnight just north of town where there'd been no swamp before. The king's sweetheart's girlfriend's lover called my mother on the phone and said she'd seen a great sharp-toothed fish cruising that impossible swamp and also how the swamp's sudden existence had ruined some of the king's oncoming real-estate ventures. In the agora my mother heard how a local fisherman had cast his net into the sea to watch it come up full of olives and there were even witnesses on hand when a toothless but handsome peasant shook an olive tree and silver minnows dropped to the ground. I wasn't anything but a boy but even I woke up one morning with a plug of seaweed in my mouth. And the politicians and the port girls and the merchants and the philosophers and the would-be loverboys and the farmers and my mother all whispered how it was fish-father Poseidon behind such portents, he who'd wanted to sneak his dominion into the actual encampment of Athens back as far as its first dawn, apparently tired once more of his lonely jurisdictions in the chambered drink. Plus, all knew Poseidon would miss no opportunity to flick his foamy beard at his book-smart niece, Athena. My mother no longer washed our clothes down at the river for fear she would look to the current and see the seahorse master himself arcing up for her from the depths. Poseidon was still fairly hot in Corinth but in Athens he'd shrunk to a trading card passed back and forth between drunk sailors and pirates and lonely merchants of salt and the occasional confused Phoenician. People lived on land and not the sea, it was just a fact, nothing to be sore about, O Poseidon. But still Poseidon wanted to encroach upon the foundational earth and maybe enlarge his fan base by lovely way of our finest girls and their shoeless feet or even a married woman sitting lonely in a windowsill or why not a couple of the smoother boys who might want to pray to the trident by force and forever with bubbles in their hair?

And we'd all heard the news of the shy schoolgirl Medusa and how that worked out.

And therefore by our betters we were encouraged, no matter which god of the big twelve to whom we professed allegiance (and only once we'd done our due diligence to our mother-father-daughter Athena), to give the earth-shaker Poseidon a little prayer, or two, so that he might not shake the earth.

—

My mother'd been born to a throwback cult family who followed the hard way of old Dionysus and she fancied the grape and she'd done her time with the maenads. The people around town who remembered her from those days grew pale and crossed to the other side of the street when they saw my mother coming. With her dark history and turbulent blood she was more like my cousin Double A than she might want to admit. In our little house there were photographs of the mother standing young with a pack of wild girls, slivery black hair in her eyes and the fibered blood of sparagmos on her hands. I treasured these photos in a troubled and perfect way. I often sneaked into my mother's room and hauled out the photo boxes she kept beneath her bed. You had to imagine the mother took part in the eating of human flesh and the concurrent or subsequent orgies without shame (I was her son and I didn't ask questions) and not all of the photos showed her tranced or homicidal. One photo in particular I enjoyed which presented her stepping over what was a human body turned inside out, my mother as a young girl, looking into the camera with a little smile on her face like she was coming to tell you her fun but terrible secret. But then she'd met my soldier father at a harvest dance over in Eleusia and he was handsome and a born hoplite who felt no fear on battlefields and he'd always been a simple and sensible Athena-first kind of guy. During the slow dances my mother confessed her bloodthirst for wine and how she'd been taught murder was a kind of love and how she preferred the fast dances over the slow. But my father'd only seen a pretty girl standing there in front of him. So my mother got pregnant with me that night in a barley field under a moon with blood on its chin and she gave up her fierce early ways for my father and as long as I'd been alive in the world, even after my father's eventual death (de-tongued on military leave by a Phrygian whoremaster), it was Athena and Athena only for my mother.

—

So, having already switched horses once, it must have been a difficult for my mother to have to pray to Poseidon.

And the gods were always and ever eavesdroppers, risky to pray to more than one of them, even in a time of emergent portent.

I remember the mother coming into my bedroom, one night around this time, worried but calm, tall like herself, her hair up for Athena. Absently she touched the old crescent scar on her forearm where one of her former blood cult victims, shortly before she'd lifted his head from his neck, had bitten her down to the bone. The wound had infected and almost killed her and now she touched at the scar in times of concern, like she did presently. She sat down on the edge of the bed and put the palm of her strong hand on my forehead and said how we would say a small word or two, that night, for the god of the seas. Normally we did our ministrations in the yard beneath the sky, with the moon up and our hands upraised and our feet dyed and decorated, but my mother didn't want to do it for Poseidon that way.

"We'll just say a small prayer here, in your bedroom, which is the lesser of the bedrooms. We'll say the prayer, also, in our normal voices, and not our big ones."

"Okay," I said.

"And we won't show our palms to the sky but we'll press them to the floor."

She stood up from the bed and I took her hand and stood and we both knelt on the floor. On the floor beside my bed I could see one of Double A's hair ties, white and silk, fallen like a moth. It must have dropped to the floor the last time she'd visited me secretly in the night. With my foot I swiffed it under the bed so my mother wouldn't see. I closed my eyes and dropped my head for prayer.

"Poseidon," my mother said, "some human beings prefer a god with a beard and you have a beard and we thank you. There are probably more seas and oceans in this world than we are aware of as a people, hence I imagine you are spread thin and we know your time is valuable. We are creatures who must drink water to survive and in some circles it is even believed we are made of water and water is your dominion. Therefore it must be that we carry you inside us. We'd prefer you wouldn't fight so much with your niece, but I have a niece myself, and I sometimes wish her ill, so I understand how you feel. Nieces can be the worst, O Poseidon. And we are sorry if you sometimes find yourself left out of our thoughts. Forgive me, forgive us. And we Greeks love our children but we know that they are not quite people yet and they are like one half of one human and though losing one is terrible," she said, reaching out for my hand, "it's also not the end of the world. A child is barely a person in fact and we are a poor family and my husband is murdered by whoremasters and buried in a foreign hog pen across the roadways of your sea and we have no money or means to make sacrifice. I'd love to have a goat on hand, for instance, or even a pheasant, how then I could turn it inside out and kill it for you lovingly. This boy here who prays beside me," said my mother, "is not a bird either, nor is he pretty, but he is my son and he is mine. He is of average intelligence and height for his age, but he's young and, when he's not busy telling lies, he's a hard worker. He is a brunette like his father. His skin is smooth under the hand and the sun, as you can see, turns it a nice color. Tomorrow I will send him down to the beach and he will stand knee-deep in the surf and he will say your name out loud for an hour. And, if it's your pleasure to do so, O Poseidon, you can take him with you to the foamy temples of the sea."

—

The next morning, before my mother went off to her job of work, which was making ceremonial headbands constantly for some approaching festival or the other (there were a lot of festivals on our little peninsula), she sent me to the beach, for to offer myself to Poseidon, like she said she would. I walked there alone with a legume sandwich in my pocket and dutifully I stood knee deep in the surf. Every minute or so, like my mother wanted, I raised up my hands and said beseechingly the name "Poseidon." A small crowd began to form on the beach behind me, the way people do, hopeful. We are creatures who really want to see a god show up. This was the public beach down near the port and some of the girls in the small crowd wore the colored arm and wristbands of Pasiphae and these girls had their hair scented by perfumes of their own concoction. They smoked cigarettes and punched each other in the shoulder for fun and pushed their cigarette butts into the sand with their bare toes and some of them knew my cousin Double A. Back when my father had been alive, he would send me down to the theater district, which was just there on the other side of the port, very near House Pasiphae and the other girl houses. In the theaters I liked to hear the plays declaimed, to look at the actors and actresses and the way they made being a human being seem grand and devastating. I would sit in the cheap seats and imagine myself the writer of one of those plays, and how I would invent believable lines for the pretty actresses to say. And they would sit in a circle around me, these actresses, and give me their best dialogue suggestions. I don't know when I learned the actresses I dreamed of weren't women but fellows in wigs and dresses, but it didn't hurt my feelings like you'd think it might. Faithfully when I closed my eyes to dream they still sat in that circle around me, blameless ladies as I imagined them, interested in their craft. So whenever I found a scrap of something to write on, I'd make my little dialogues and hope for what fame might be. I was big on storylines with unlikely twosomes being stuck adrift at sea or manning the same lone watchtower. And I looked forward to those theater days when my father, home on leave, would call me over to him, pretend to find a coin behind my ear. He'd have been at the ongoing wars and would want to spend some time alone with the ex-maenad mother. And I was happy to be gotten rid of and happy that my parents loved each other and I'd run off with my coin to the port and the little theater by the sea.

But eager as I was, I always thought it better to take the long way there, as the short way took me right past the House of Pasiphae.

—

In those days, back when my cousin Double A's mother was still alive and Double A was being perfumed and trained for a marriage that never happened to her, the girls of House Pasiphae frightened me. Not only the girls of House Pasiphae but also of the other houses, Nephele Rising, Europa, Europa, the Ox and the Skirt. The port widows who ran these houses corralled the girls in-of-doors and out of the sun as much as possible, to keep their skin light and soft, but, whenever there were plays running, the port widows would let the girls out, as a little reward, to relax and watch the procession of theatergoers. They'd sit like as many birds out on the roof in their white dresses and barefoot and beneath their elevated hairstyles they'd jingle the metal bands on their wrists and they'd flirt with and hoot at passersby. You would walk by them and they'd tell you things about yourself that made you sad, especially if you were a boy. They'd tell you how it was your mother who made the shorts you were wearing. I didn't understand how that would be an insult exactly, yet it still hurt my feelings. They'd flick lit cigarettes at you and say they were sorry, but you could tell they didn't mean it. They'd inform you you were somehow shorter than you were the last time you walked past. They'd say hearty embarrassing things that made you blush and that you didn't always understand and one of them might baaaa like a sheep as you went by.

—

But that was a while ago and I was taller now and my cousin Double A was now one of these house girls, a new inductee, yes, but well respected for her beauty and height. And secondhand I'd gained a little respect by way of being her cousin and I even learned the names of some of these girls and they didn't scare me as much anymore. One of them, in fact, this short girl everyone called Urse, was even a friend of mine. Urse had sharp eyes and a little upturned nose and superstitious blond hair, so blond it was white, like spun bone. And the girl Urse was one of the house girls sitting on the beach behind me, in the crowd that day, while I did what my mother wanted and stood knee-deep in the surf waiting for the god Poseidon to abduct me. And I was just about to call it quits when the girl Urse waded out with her dress lifted from the foam and stood next to me.

I looked over at her and then we looked out at the ocean.

"Mama's boy," she said.

"Urse," I said.

The girl leaned over and made a big deal of looking under an incoming wave.

"Looks like Poseidon's a no show," she said.

"Looks like," I said.

She passed me her cigarette and I drew from it and tried not to cough.

"There's a party night after tomorrow," she said. "Some rich kid's house. After the Eleusinian Mysteries."

From the bib pocket of her dress she produced a little piece of paper and gave it to me and it was the address for the party, but written out in Double A's handwriting, a heart beneath the phrase "meet me there."

I put the piece of paper in my pocket.

About the party I said to the girl Urse, "Are you going?"

"If I can get loose," she said.

I nodded. Urse changed the subject.

"The other day," she said, "when some of us snuck down here, there was a woman trying to push her baby out to sea. She had this little raft she'd made out of driftwood and things. She was crying but the baby was real peaceful. And the mother would say a word or two of offering. But the waves kept pushing the baby back to the beach."

"That makes me sad for some reason," I said.

Urse nodded and we stood there agreeing how it was sad. Then I half turned to look behind me and saw the crowd was breaking up, people standing, shaking the sand off their blankets, dusting it off their bottoms, people no longer interested in me now that Poseidon wasn't going to take the bait. They hadn't seen what they wanted to see. Somewhere in there I felt bad to have disappointed them. A tentacle of seaweed wrapped itself around the girl Urse's ankle and she leaned against me and lifted her leg to untangle herself.

"How's Double A?" I asked.

"She's good," she said. "She would've snuck down with me, but they started her learning shoes today. Then the widows had her in the back rooms doing practice with hugs."

"How does that work?" I asked.

"If you have nice feet," Urse said, "they teach you how to wear shoes."

"I mean with the hugging," I said.

She made a wry face.

"They've got this male dummy they use," she said.

I nodded as if that made sense and I turned and Urse turned and we started walking back up the beach together.

"You wouldn't think a pretty girl like Double A would need to practice hugging," Urse said.

"I suppose not," I said.

Urse accidentally-on-purpose bumped into me.

"You know a thing or two about her hugs," she said, "or am I guessing?"

—

A schoolgirl I knew got carried off to Olympus by a tornado, but a small tornado, a tornado only as big as a man and—according to at least one witness—the tornado was not only the size of a man, but even took the shape of one, even seemed to walk, to speak. Zeus, probably. Some said it was a little waterspout and not a tornado and those people thought it was Poseidon instead of Zeus. And then there was the time, in separate incidents, where two kids, one a male and one a female, disappeared on the same day, opposite ends of town, both turned into flowers, one a snapdragon, the other, I think, a dandelion. Some said Apollo, others said Hermes. It was hard to keep track of all the new flowers. Then it was the several kids who grew bark for skin and had to stand still for eternity in forests. Then one young soldier accidentally saw the goddess Artemis bathing and had his eyes pecked out by a huge crow who then flew his eyes up and out of the universe of the world and directly into the sun. In fact there were so many stories about the goddess Artemis being seen while taking a bath that it was starting to seem like she should be more careful. And there was a helot girl I had a crush on who turned up dead in a river, maybe Poseidon, or maybe old Proteus. The girl had been reported as having a special friendship with an alligator gar—this was one of the reasons I liked her, that she had a kind feeling for animals—an alligator gar that swam up to her beneath the bridge one day and asked her for her name, which was Alexa. When they found Alexa's body it was said that her eyes were open and she had a single snow-white fish scale in her mouth. And this isn't counting all the kids who just disappeared or whose bodies bobbed up in a well and afterward they didn't get turned into anything interesting and no one ever told a story about them.

—

And even I, at least according to my mother, had had such an encounter, not as dramatic, not as terrible.

Once, not too far back, there was an old beggar woman who sometimes worked the street outside my mother's house. On this day my mother asked me to clean the kitchen while she was at work. I'd just mopped the kitchen floor and thought I'd open the shutters to let the breeze play through. I poked my head out to look up at the sun and I saw the old beggar woman leaning unsteadily against our gate. As I watched I could see how she looked over to notice how I was watching her. Then she clutched at the gate pole and fell down.

I ran out the front door and into the yard.

"Are you all right?"

The old woman looked at me with clouding eyes and her voice had a hollow place, like she would be able to hide things inside it. "You're a kind boy," she said.

I held out my hand to help her up but she pushed my hand away. "I guess I'll just sit right here if that's okay," she said.

"It's fine."

She said, "I wonder if I could trouble you for a drink of water?"

"Just one second," I said.

I went back to the house and into the kitchen, poured some water from the pitcher into an earthen cup. I looked around the kitchen. My mother had put aside a couple of sardines and some bread and cheese niblets for my lunch. I took a hunk of the bread and laid a sardine out on it and took this with the cup of water back to the old woman.

"This is more than I asked for," she said.

"There's some cheese inside if you'd like some."

The old woman touched at her stomach.

"I'm not too friendly with cheese," she said.

She drank the water, handed up the cup to me. Her eyes cleared when she regarded the sardine and I watched as like a pelican she seemed to swallow the sardine whole. Then she folded the greasy bread in half and put it in her dress pocket for later. She seemed much better then and she held out her hand for me to help her up and I pulled her up and she came up easily, quickly. Too quickly. Suddenly her face was in mine and she kissed me on the lips. It scared me at first, to be kissed by a beggar woman who was old as two mothers or more, to feel that little bit of tongue, but her mouth tasted good, not like sardines but sugary, like vanilla.

"You've done me this beautiful kindness," the old woman said.

She put her arms around my neck.

"Don't mention it," I said.

She stood there, too close, looking into my face. I'd judged her to be shorter, but we stood eye to eye. A weird calm fell over me.

"What's your name?" she asked.

I searched my head and couldn't find a name in there.

"I don't know."

"If it's okay with you," she said, "I'll just call you sweetheart."

"Okay."

She smiled and her teeth were fresh and white. I was about to say something—I have no idea what—but then she winked and said, much unlike the few old ladies I have known, "Catch you later, sweetheart."

And then she turned and walked off up the road.

With the empty cup in hand I walked back toward the house, feeling uneasy about the whole thing.

Later, when my mother came home, I told her about it.

"No doubt one of the goddesses," my mother said, "or maybe a cross-dressed Zeus."

I touched my fingertips to my lips where the old woman had kissed me.

My mother wrinkled up her nose.

"I can still smell the vanilla on you," she said.

—

At the rich kid's afterparty there were no grownups and I looked around for my cousin Double A, couldn't find her amongst the revelers, not her nor the girl Urse. The house was two levels with a grotto-like wading pool out front and the whole place smelled like silphium and the second level had a nice long wraparound balcony fashioned with railings of salt cedar painted harbor white. You could see the flash of this railing when you approached the house, even in the dark like I did, from all the way down the block. And of the house's huge living area let me say there were enough pillar candles burning in the windows that you thought you'd entered a place of worship. Sliding hand-carved plane-wood doors opened onto a backyard where a pair of large fig trees stood polite and bough-heavy and green. When you stood beneath these trees you could almost hear them breathing. It was worth the risk of sneaking out of my mother's house to see these trees. I went from the trees out around to the front of the house and I lurked near the wading pool and then I went into the house and walked from room to room, trying to blend in. These were all the children of the rich and I'd worried I would look out of place among them, but it turns out they were all trying to dress like kids down near the port, so I didn't stand out. To further blend in I picked up a glass of clear liquor from the refreshment table and I took it into the living room with me, found a corner and stood in it. The living room had been refashioned as a dance floor and I watched the dances. The music was one kid humming and another kid on a drum. I took a drink of the drink in my hand and it tasted like licorice with eyes on it.

—

A girl in a pink poorboy's tunic came up to me like she knew who I was. She had short blond hair and she held a half-eaten fig between her thumb and forefinger and she was drunk.

"You're friends with Dmitri," she said.

I didn't know the person she was talking about.

"I don't know who you're talking about."

"Don't lie to me."

"Yes, I know Dmitri," I said.

"Have you seen him around?"

"No," I said.

She looked at me with suspicion.

"He was just here," she said.

"Maybe out back," I said.

She bopped the half-eaten fig at me.

"I was just out back," she said.

"I don't know what to say," I said.

"Tell Dmitri," the blond girl said, "I know he's fucking around. Tell him I know he thinks he's smart."

—

I lost track of the dancing until I heard what sounded like a fight breaking out on the dance floor, a couple of boys pushing each other and name calling and then a couple of more joined in. The liquor felt like a little sun rising in my stomach and the principals stripped themselves down and someone brought in a vial of oil and they oiled themselves up and the girls floated out to the edges of the living room and this was how the dance floor turned into a wrestling ring. Bodies hit the floor and the pillar candles jumped in the windowsills and it was no longer my kind of scene and I headed up the stairs to the second level where it might be quieter. As I went up the stairs the girl in the pink poorboy tunic was coming down and she gave me the same suspicious eye and asked me again if I'd seen the boy Dmitri. I lied again and I told her, yes, I'd seen Dmitri, just now, out front by the wading pool. The girl scowled and went down and I made the landing and there weren't many people upstairs. I turned into the hall and I wandered from room to empty room. It was a fine house and I knew there was probably a bathtub up there and I wanted to take a look at it. I didn't ever find the tub but—even better—I walked into a room that seemed to be a family library. On the unpainted shelves (cedar again, I think) you saw the scrolls, white or yellowing, each looped around a knobbed cylinder and hanging on gilt hooks screwed into the wood. Without candles it was the dark of moonlight throughout the second level and I thought I would like to inspect a scroll or two—I'd only seen scrolls like that on the stage of the port theater, unrolled and read from by actors—so I stepped to the near shelf so that I might get a closer look. Doing so, I put my foot down on what felt like someone's stomach. It was some kids there, on the floor, making out beneath a blanket in the library. I hadn't seen them. I withdrew my foot and one of the kids poked his rumpled head out and then the other kid poked her rumpled head out. Then there was a third kid and he poked his rumpled head out.

And this third kid looked up and said to me, "This is so embarrassing for you."

—

I apologized and turned to go out the same door I thought I'd come in.

Except it was a different door and now I found myself standing outside, in the open air, on a balcony.

It was not the large wraparound I'd seen coming up the hill to the house, but a private alcove-like balcony with a brass rail and view of the backyard and the two incredible fig trees and then the trees of a small forest in the distance and over there and beyond it all the sea. I stepped out and let the door shut behind me. There was a bench out there and I imagined in the morning you'd select a scroll from the library and sit on the bench to peruse your scroll in a quantity of natural light. I sat on the bench and I looked into the moonlit backyard and I thought things over. I figured Urse and Double A hadn't been able to escape the House of Pasiphạe, that or they'd just forgotten about the party altogether. I thought I'd wait a little longer, in case they showed up. If not, I'd head back home, be safe in bed well before the rosy-fingered dawn, etc. I didn't want to have to sneak back through the library and past the kids beneath the blanket and I wondered if I couldn't just jump from the balcony without hurting myself. I couldn't take my eyes off those fig trees but I must have unconsciously seen or felt a shadow or a flash in my peripheral. I turned my head to the right. And just down a little, across the way, same level, same shape and same configuration as mine, was another balcony, about thirty feet from me. Twin alcove balconies, one on each end of the backside of the house, mine and the other. And there, standing in profile on the other balcony, she was: Double A in a shoulders-free white dress, her back to the brass rail and her upper body arched dangerously back over it, her face pointed up to the moon. She was smoking a cigarette and she had her dress lifted to her chin. Kneeling before her was another person, dark-headed and slim and male, head bobbing between Double A's legs. Like a stork she had one foot planted on the boy's shoulder and the foot was lovely in a white shoe with straps. She blew a smoke ring up at the moon. She glanced over and I saw from the movement of her head she was drunk. She saw me and raised her eyebrows and mimed a surprised face. She pointed down at the head bobbing between her legs and stage-whispered across the space between us, "This is my friend, Dmitri."

—

I waited until Double A called the coast clear and then I worked my way through the dark second level and then around finally to the other balcony. Double A introduced me to a blushing Dmitri and we shook hands and he was a small lovely boy who looked like a creature of the forest, except hairless. I told the boy Dmitri how there was a girl in a pink poorboy tunic looking for him and he kissed Double A on the cheek worriedly and slipped off back into the house. Double A rolled her eyes and I leaned against the rail and Double A leaned against the rail and we looked out at the backyard.

"I'm glad you made it," she said. "I was just about to be mad at you."

"Downstairs it's fallen to wrestling," I said.

My cousin laughed and leaned her head against my shoulder.

"Your feet look good in shoes," I said.

"They feel weird but I like them," she said.

"Urse didn't make it out?"

"The port widows got her." She sighed. "I don't want to go back to Pasiphae's tonight. You think I can stay at your mom's?"

"If we're quiet," I said.

"And I think you don't even," she said, "seem too upset with me." She looked over. She was talking about me seeing her with Dmitri.

"No," I said.

"Good," she said.

"Angela," I said.

"Shut up," she said.

—

After that, things went quickly. I may have again told Double A how beautiful her feet looked in the white shoes. Double A may have told me it was sweet that Dmitri didn't bother me but if it had been the other way around she might have to murder me. We talked about maybe stealing a scroll from the library. We definitely heard an uptick in the thumps and rattles of the wrestling downstairs, thought it was nothing, but then there was a scream where it didn't sound like wrestling anymore. Double A and I stood from the balcony bench simultaneously. You couldn't tell if it was a boy or a girl screaming. And then it was the seagull sound of many boys and girls screaming and we looked out over the rail to see kids fleeing the house into the yard. I thought maybe one of the pillar candles had caught the house on fire until one kid came out of the house, not running like the others, but thrown, end over end, like a stick. He landed, with his neck crooked, in a little pile on the grass. He landed next to a terrified girl who then stopped running to look down at the body and just stood there shaking, like she'd been struck by invisible lighting.

Double A yelled down to the girl, "What's going on?"

The girl turned. Her unfocused eyes climbed up and found us. "Poseidon," she said calmly. "Kids are drowning in that house."

—

Double A seemed ready to say something more to the girl, but a three-pronged spear of white light came from the house and hit the girl in the face, the center prong sinking between her eyes with a jolt, gigging her head into the pine tree behind her. Then the white spear of light pulsed so brightly I had to shut my eyes. When I opened them the spear had disappeared and there was nothing left of the girl but her silhouette smoked into the bark of the tree. Kids kept coming out of the house, some running, some flung. Like the house was a wineskin, water came pouring out into the backyard, reddish from what you understood was blood. I turned and opened the door going from the balcony back into the house. Double A grabbed my arm.

"No," she said. "We need to go over."

—

She pulled me back and I turned toward the rail and got one foot up. Behind us came a walloping sound like something huge coming up the stairs and the eaves shook and there was another scream, closer this time. I turned and looked back into the dark of the house to see a blond girl burst through the door. I thought it was the girl in pink from before, Dmitri's friend, but it was a different girl, this one with watery blood soaking her dress. This blond came running toward us and I turned toward the rail Double A had already gone over. I followed and hit the ground and looked up at the balcony just as the blond girl stepped up onto the balcony rail. She was scared and might not jump and Double A hollered up at her to do it already. As the girl jumped a large white hand closed around her neck to pull her back. Her body jerked like a puppet and she hung in midair and then her body came down without its head anymore. The body spilled to my feet like laundry. And then the girl's blond head came flying over the rail like flung from a sling and it was Poseidon standing there, looking not unlike a man, water burbling up behind him and spilling over the rail. He looked down at me and then his eyes settled on Double A and he smiled at Double A and then Double A and I turned and ran toward the distant trees.

—

We sat on the bed in my room, back in my mother's house, not saying anything.

Through the wall I could hear my mother breathing deeply.

The sun changed places with the moon, just outside the window, and Double A lifted her dress over her head.

"Take off your clothes," she said.

I stood up and I stumbled, a little, doing what she asked.

"That girl's head," Double A said as she watched me undress, "is probably a meteor by now."

We both laughed, not at the girl so much, I guess, but for how simple it was to be dead. I left my clothes on the floor and climbed onto the bed. Double A pulled her hair up thoughtfully and tied it high and palmed herself forward to me, her legs crossed under her. She helped me get into her lap, facing her. I wrapped my legs around her waist and my arms around her neck. She was who she was and I closed my eyes and I was me and someone else. I imagined myself lying on my back in a barley field, just like my mother had done it, except as a boy, being made pregnant beneath a moon with blood on its chin.

"Open your eyes," Double A said.

I opened my eyes and looked at her.

Would her head have to become a meteor? Will her body be shot into stars?

Of course, came the answer, *yes, forever, hurry.*

THE GHOST OF TRACY VALENTIC

She'd been a second-string cheerleader high on white crosses and she'd been my babysitter and she'd also been (though no one knew except my father) going to motels with my father.

When she walked she had a way of trailing her hands along, like she was touching at tall flowers or the heads of small invisible children who walked with her.

On her ankle was the usual twenty-dollar butterfly.

The suicide note was a letter she sent to my father, straightforward in tone and factual and with no handwringing, an actual line in it that said, "I don't think you know what's right."

—

When implicated in such a letter a father goes East to start a new life, a mother sits out back all night at the firepit, drinking pitcher cocktails and having arguments with opponents who aren't really there. The father gets into real estate. The mother wins each argument.

—

The ghost of Tracy Valentic showed up one night, in my bed. The dream I was having was going to be my first wet dream, I could tell, and it was a dream where I was floating naked in a parasailing rig—the view was of me looking down between my feet—over a brownish lake, the lake full of huge, lazy serpents with shiny skin colored in a pink and green camouflage pattern. In this dream of the serpents and the parasailing rig, I'd started to circle down toward the surface of the lake. I could tell what was going to happen and I didn't want to have the rest of the dream. I felt like having the wet dream to completion would be like going through a door into a room where people were saying bad things about me. I'd been fearful of the serpents and I'd put my feet out, helplessly, to stop myself, which is when one of the serpents happened to break the surface of the lake. I pushed my feet off of the serpent's pink and green back to stay airborne and I'd come in midair, feeling not like it was my doing but as if it had been pulled out of me, like a magician's scarf, with the slime of the serpent greasy on the bottoms of my feet. I'd woken up with my feet cold and there was the ghost of Tracy Valentic, my former babysitter, looking at me, her eyes dark green instead of the brown that I'd remembered. "I sure missed you," she said, four weeks dead.

—

"Who's in your grave?" I asked the ghost of Tracy Valentic. I think I thought I was still in the dream, where such a question seemed appropriate.

"What's the question again?" she asked.

"Who's in your grave?" I said.

"Tracy Valentic is in my grave," the ghost of Tracy Valentic answered.

—

I only saw her a few more times. Once when I was peeing she slid back the shower curtain and said to me, "A woman doesn't like to be buried," and then I'd say about three months later she showed up, while I was looking around the kitchen for a snack, the ghost of Tracy Valentic leaning against the refrigerator, finishing the thought she'd begun three months earlier. "A woman prefers to be raptured," she said.

—

The last time I saw her was the nicest time I saw her. I'm in the bathroom. I'm not afraid of her anymore. I'm about to go to bed. I look down to wet the toothbrush and I look up into the mirror and there she is, this time standing right behind me. "While brushing your teeth," she says, "remember to take your time. You could read a little from a magazine article," she says, putting whatever her hand is made of on my shoulder, "you could take a stroll around the house. You could make a mental to-do list for the next morning. This ensures," says the ghost of Tracy Valentic, "a sustained brushing of the teeth. This ensures you will have happy teeth for the rest of your life."

TRAILER PARK GOTHIC

Sister Rae and I are half-siblings, but I don't care. Sister Rae's father is my mother's ex-husband. My father (whoever you are) was just this random man from an internet scenario, from back in the bad old days, when my mother was married to Sister Rae's father. Before he went off to Texas ("To start a cult or something," Mom said), Sister Rae's father had had some strange ideas about love, one of which was he wanted to watch another man have sex with his wife, which apparently my mother had gone along with, young wife that she was at twenty-two or however old, or maybe she'd even liked the guy. I wasn't too clear on the details. I am alive and can't blame anyone.

—

I was little when Sister Rae had been the one to spill this secret. This was still when we lived in the trailer near the Wabash, not the trailer we live in now. You could smell the floodplain when the river was low, which worked on everyone's nerves. Teenage Rae had me in her lap in front of the television, mad at my mother about something, and Rae just said it out loud about how there were different fathers and why.

"And this is what happens," Rae said, loud enough Mom would hear it, "when you get the internet involved."

Mom stuck her head in from the bedroom area, where she'd been on the phone, her eyes wide.

"Did I just hear you say the word 'cuckold'?" Mom asked Rae.

"You must have," said Sister Rae.

"Jesus Christ," Mom said. "Why are you explaining fathers to him?"

—

But I remember that night, how it ended up, as a good night. The two women made up and Mom told me I wasn't all that traumatized. They sat me between and we watched an old black and white movie where aliens burn an Arctic outpost. Mom liked the black and whites. I started to fade, even with the movie as scary as it was, even with my paternity made suddenly bizarre, my head going into one woman's lap and my feet into the other's.

I think it was Sister Rae who carried me to bed that night. And I slept for a while, alone back there, but of course I had dreams of tall and perverse fathers, or maybe not dreams, but visions, sightings. So I came back out to the tv area, hoping to be told by Sister Rae and Mom that I wasn't one of these men I dreamed of. And I looked at Sister Rae on the couch, my mother sitting on the floor with her back to the couch, doing Sister Rae's toes, them watching more alien mayhem on the television, lost looks on both their faces, the screen popping up tiny in their eyes. My mother had stuck those little green foam toe spreaders on my sister's feet, which made Rae's toes look like they were going to prison, and I felt full of love to see these women, right there where I'd last seen them, alive and not in a dream, being themselves in reality, almost twins in the light of the tv. They turned and looked at me. And in footed pajamas I said to these two women who were mine, "I don't care who anyone's father is."

—

Early on, I couldn't tell these two women apart, or I didn't want to, two pretty women with dark hair and gaps in their teeth, high foreheads and a slight Morticia look to each, both of them my mother as far as I cared to tell the difference, both looking down at me with smiles or frowns, coming at me with a hairbrush and pretending I would be a heartbreaker.

—

What I miss most about that time of the trailer near the Wabash was being carried from here to there by two women in the night. There were only two beds in the trailer, both in the back past the bathroom. Mom slept in one, Sister Rae in the other, the little gap between. Whenever I fell asleep on the couch, one of the women had to carry me back and lay me down into either one of the beds. Then when the women finally got sleepy, they'd come in again and pick me up from the bed, carry me from the bed and back out onto the couch, which was where I officially slept. Space was at a premium, Mom said, just like in New York City. Most mornings I woke up on the couch with this vague feeling of having been shuffled, ferried across tile and carpet by women in the night, Mom carrying me in, Rae carrying me out, but sometimes Sister Rae or Mom—too tired or too high to move me—would just plop into whichever bed along with me, and I'd wake up with Mom in the big bed or with Sister Rae in the narrow bed. Or Mom would be late waiting tables at Conrad's Supper Club, which is when Sister Rae would leave me in Mom's bed, and I'd feel Mom slide tired under the covers, smelling like popovers and whatever fried special, telling me to close my eyes and hush. With Mom I'd usually sleep solid and wake up in the morning holding hands or touching knees, though sleeping with Sister Rae, on those nights when Sister Rae would come home late from boyfriend one or boyfriend two, was like sleeping with a knife fight. Sister Rae had a strong and apparent dream life. Sometimes her dream would tell her how I was an assailant. She'd push away at my face with her hands, pinning my head to the wall. Sometimes I'd wake up sore and bent feeling. But then on the other hand sometimes Rae's dream logic would tell her to protect me, and she'd hold me doll-tight, like we had our backs to a cliff, until it was hard for me to breathe, which was my favorite.

—

That was a while ago and now Mom waits tables at a restaurant in Evansville, a little more upscale, called Malley O's. We are trailered in a rental park outside of town. My friend the next trailer over is a blond girl named Juliet Hudok and sometimes we each tell each other hi. Sister Rae would live with us, normally, but she's been up in Vincennes, at the Teen Village. Out in the dangerous world Sister Rae had been high, on a couch in an abandoned house, where some meth-related violence occurred. Someone had put a turkey bone into someone else's eye. Someone else shot into the face of the one who had used the turkey bone as a weapon. Her boyfriend at the time—I think his name was actually Ray, with a Y—had been one of the chief offenders.

So the judge sent Sister Rae to Teen Village for meth and for consorting. My mother said to me, "That's your sister, Rae. Everyone in the country is high on opioids, but Rae is sticking to her roots." This being Mom's way of admitting to some guilt about Sister Rae, since Mom herself had struggled here and there with a meth addiction as a lass ("lass" being Mom's word for what she was back then), though I never heard Sister Rae blame anyone but Sister Rae about it.

—

The night before we were supposed to go pick up Sister Rae from Teen Village, Mom's boyfriend Alf came over. This was in the other trailer, now, the one in Evansville, and I was older. A few words, then, about Alf. Alf was a quiet and serious man, younger than my mother. They met at Malley O's, which was farm to table. Alf took graduate classes in the English department. Mom would kid Alf about it: "Why isn't there an American department?" she'd ask, though Alf would think she was being serious and more than likely choose to explain it to her. And I thought at first that Alf seemed like an okay guy, even though he couldn't recognize a joke and was balding prematurely in a way that looked like an affliction, even though he didn't seem to like me and my being underfoot obviously made him nervous. Not that balding makes you a bad person, it's about the way you react to it. I believe Alf was mad at his scalp most days. It didn't seem to allow him to enjoy much. Nor did Alf like to come to the mother's trailer very often. You could tell Alf liked pretending his local waitress girlfriend (my mom) wasn't a single mother, just a hot-looking trailer thing he would educate with his presence. I think I and Sister Rae—particularly Sister Rae, going on seventeen—kind of spoiled the illusion for him, or caused him a guilt of some kind. He would look at me with a pained expression whenever I was around. Same reason, I suppose, that Alf didn't like it that my mother knew, by heart, most *all* of the famous soliloquys of Shakespeare, which her grandmother had taught her to memorize. Hard to educate someone who could do most all of Hamlet's solos. I never knew my mom's grandmother but her name was Katarine and she must have been quite a gal, come over from old Bohemia, speaking no English, but by the time she'd died having taught her granddaughter the best poems in the language.

Mom had done Rosalind in high school and there was a video of it we sometimes watched. You didn't want to watch that video, or else risk having to fall in love with a second, younger version of her. Mom tried to teach some of the soliloquys to me, thinking maybe I'd like the theater, but I wasn't much for being out in front of people, plus I couldn't focus on anything but Mom's face when she did the parts. She'd change her voice. Sometimes she'd find props near at hand to use. I gave up learning the words and I became her audience. I'd sit on the carpet and watch her go, my mouth wide open. I thought she was such a good actress that it scared me Hollywood agents would come to the trailer to take her away from me in limousines. Her Cleopatra was fast and sly, but it wasn't even my favorite. I can't remember the name of the play now, but the one where the girl dresses up as a boy and wakes up near a headless man's body: I asked for that one all the time. Mom would touch the back of her hand to her forehead and fall back on the couch, actual tears in her eyes.

"Oh Posthumus, alas," she would say, "where is thy head?"

—

I guess I'm about twelve at this time and I don't remember how it happened or what, but I'm awake and already pissing my boxer briefs in the kitchen area, looking at Mom on the floor, her mouth cracked in a grin but all bloody, the man Alf reeling over her, shaking his hand like it was on fire, saying, "You broke my hand, you stupid cunt," which was a thing, "stupid cunt," I'd heard my mother and Sister Rae call each other, but it sounded different in that context, particularly coming from Alf, who usually tried to talk in cultured tones, plus Mom bleeding and Alf obviously drunk where I'd not seen him drunk before. So I just pretended Alf was the stranger he actually was and lowered my head as a ram and rushed at his crotch. Mostly it felt like a strong wind picked me up and there I went sailing into the tv stand, time enough before the tv toppled onto me to look up and see my mom in the meantime had found a steak knife, saying to Alf how if he didn't leave she'd turn his balls loose.

—

Mom got some ice on her eye for a bit and then said fuck it and put on some red heart-shaped sunglasses belonging to Sister Rae. In the sunglasses she looked like Sister Rae so much that it almost panicked me, how two people could be so similar.

I looked at my face in the bathroom mirror and I could see some of my mother and Sister Rae in there, particularly around the eyes, though my nose got in between the eyes and ruined the effect. I had my genetics straight by then and I knew I was related as much to Mom as Sister Rae was, but they looked so much alike, plus me being the boy, that I often felt like the odd one.

In the bathroom Mom stripped me of the wet boxers and turned me here and there to look for damage I might have sustained going into the tv stand or the tv coming down on me. She kidded me saying how the television would have smashed if it hadn't fallen on top of me, so I was the true hero of the incident, but I could tell she hated I'd had to see all that. She took some slugs from the bottle of vodka she kept in the freezer and we got into bed together, collecting ourselves, her breath hot with the alcohol, the storm of all that violence passing so quickly it made Mom kind of goofy in the absence of it. She had her phone in bed with us in case Alf would return in his Subaru, but he didn't.

We watched a black and white off her phone, which she balanced on her chest, one of the movies with the blond Carole Lombard playing dumb in it, but you could see, around the corners of the ridiculous things Carole Lombard was saying, how quick she really was. Or this is what Mom told me, that and how Carole Lombard died in a plane crash on her way to do a charity event. We watched for a while the doomed Carole Lombard and Mom asked me what I thought she, herself, would look like blond. The thought of Mom blond had never occurred to me, that her hair was the color it was because she let it be that color.

I tried to keep as close to Mom's body as I could. And when I started to drift off Mom said, "You're growing up in a weird situation, kiddo."

And I said, "I don't mind it."

She poked me in the ribs. "If you're ever thinking of becoming a serial killer, try to give us a little heads up on it."

—

I can see my own trouble with drugs and I can see making drug money doing blowjobs at rest areas like it happens to kids, but I wouldn't become a serial killer. You can feel that kind of thing pretty early, I hope, what you're capable of. I could sense certain fuckups forming in me, gearing up, but Shakespeare and Carole Lombard and Sister Rae would bring me back before I got too far off into the horizon where you're keeping the hair of ladies in a box beneath your bed. Not to mention the mother, bent steak knife in her hand, able to keep at least some of it at bay. Or anyway this is along the lines of what I was thinking, the next morning, waiting for Mom to get ready for the trip to Teen Village for the gathering up of Sister Rae. I walked from the trailer over to the common picnic/playground area they had in the park, just killing time, certain and proud I would never murder anyone. I hung from the overhead bars a while, just staring off toward the tree line. At one of the picnic tables, between the tetanus jungle gym and a lazy tetherball pole, I saw the blond girl and trailer park friend, Juliet Hudok, watching me. The Hudok girl lived just a trailer over from ours. Now she was sitting at the picnic table smoking a cigarette, looking pale and light like something the wind had blown in. Juliet's mother had run off some time back. Juliet lived in the trailer with her father, a guy who worked third shift over at CBS. On his days off this father sat in front of his trailer in a lawn chair, presiding, drinking tall boys and staring at my mother and sister a lot, drinking and telling anyone who passed him by how pretty soon he meant to put on a barbeque for the whole trailer park, though he never did put on a barbeque.

I dropped off the overheads and walked over. Juliet nodded her head at me. There'd been a Jonah fish fry a couple of evenings before and somehow near the picnic tables it still smelled like codfish grease. I sat down at the picnic table across from Juliet. The cigarette she smoked had greenish writing near the filter. She had a couple of forgotten Barbie dolls on the table in front of her and she blew smoke over their bodies at me.

"Some excitement over at yours last night," Juliet said.

"Yeah," I said.

Juliet said, "I didn't think a Subaru could burn rubber like that."

I nodded. "Alf," I said.

"Goodbye, Alf," Juliet said.

I looked down at the dolls on the table. Juliet had the dolls on top of each other, head to feet. One was the male doll but he was wearing a dress. One was one of the woman dolls and it hadn't any clothes on. She looked at me look at the dolls and she asked, "Is your sister back yet?" She picked a bit of tobacco from her tongue and frowned at it between her fingertips.

"We're going to pick her up today," I said.

"I think your sister is so pretty," Juliet said. "And your mother, my god."

—

Sister Rae came out pale and chubby and she flopped into the passenger seat of Mom's Malibu. When she got into the car she carried the disinfectant smell of Teen Village in her hair. She said to Mom and I, first thing, "It's *really* hard to not want to do drugs right now."

"I know, baby," Mom said. She brought a joint out from her purse and she lit it, right there in the parking lot of Teen Village, and passed it to Sister Rae. "It's not like real drugs or anything," Mom said. Sister Rae smiled. The two women smoked in the front seat and we all three sat there looking at Teen Village. From the name of the place I was half expecting, I don't know, a kind of theme-park look. But it was square and deadly there, poised on the edge of its parking lot. An old woman sat out front on a bench with her hands clasped in her lap and her eyes wide. I didn't want to know what was going on in her head. Mom lowered her sunglasses and showed Sister Rae the shiner Alf had given her. Sister Rae touched gently with her fingertips the swelling beneath Mother's eye and the crease in Mom's lip. Sister Rae blew a plume of smoke past Mom's head and said old-fashionedly, "That no good so and so."

—

As we made the city limits of Evansville, Mom reminded herself how she liked to shop for groceries while high and veered off at Kreitler's for wine coolers and some chicken breasts to grill when we got back to the trailer. I sat in the back seat, listening to Sister Rae talk, watching Mom float into the grocery store like on clouds. "First I'm going to have to shave my legs for about four years," Sister Rae said. She took the roach from the Malibu's ashtray and scooted down low in the seat with it. She got it lit and got her bare feet up on the dash and watched herself wiggle her toes. "Then I don't know what," Rae said, "maybe take a good hard look at some pornography, get a job at the public library, think about moving to Florida, lose some of this detention weight, see if any lesbians might date me."

—

Mom cooked the chicken on the grill in the picnic area, a little bottled barbeque sauce and some pinches of this and that she threw in, pretending it was secret, Mom in the cutoffs and the white halter that completed what she called her summer look. I'd walk a wine cooler out to her from the trailer every now and then. She took the heart-shaped shades off and she put them on me. The mouse under her eye had settled. In the low trailer park light you couldn't tell much had happened to her. From a distance she looked enough like a girl that it made your heart jump, the smoke from the chicken following her around. Sister Rae kept going into the trailer and then coming back out, wearing a different dress each time, seeing about the fit, for Sister Rae had missed her dresses when at Teen Village. Eventually Rae settled in on a yellow one with white lace around the bib, just a touch too tight for her, the yellow against her black hair giving her a bit of a bumblebee vibe. She played some country music off her phone and I sat down next to her on the trailer step, making up dumb lyrics. She hooked her arm around my neck and called me dillweed. Mom came from the grill after a while with the tongs in one hand and the pan of scorched chicken in the other, smiling, walking that way she did when barefoot and a little drunk, eyes down at the grass and careful, like she didn't want to surprise anything.

Which is about when Juliet Hudok's old man came out from his trailer. It was his day off and his day for drinking and fantasy barbecues. I watched him unfold his lawn chair and sit down with a cooler of tallboys next to him. He looked three sheets already and it took him a while unfolding the chair, like it was technology new to him. He had a half pint of something in his front shirt pocket. He sat there, drinking, looking back and forth at my mom and at my sister, looking off back toward the loop road like he wasn't looking at my mom and at my sister, his eyes bleary and taking too long to catch up with the movements of his head.

—

After we ate, Sister Rae and Mom watched Boris Karloff on the couch and messed around on their phones. I'd been sneaking drinks off their wine coolers all night and I lay on the floor with a pillow under my head, forgetting there was a world beyond me, trying to focus on the plot, feeling the hum of the little A/C unit in my teeth. Mom got up and stepped across me and poked her toe into my bellybutton and then went toward the fridge, but she stopped at the trailer door and looked out. She said, "That little blond girl's just sitting out there."

—

By this time, Juliet's father had gone back into the trailer and blond Juliet, his daughter, had must have come out. I got up from the floor and went over to where Mom was, looking out the screen. Sister Rae came up behind me. Juliet sat out at a picnic table, smoking, same place I'd run across her that morning. You could see the white flare of her hair in the dark and the little orange dot of the cigarette's cherry, the lightning flash of her cell phone on her downturned face.

"That asshole," my mom said.

"Let me go see about the girl," Sister Rae said.

—

After a bit Sister Rae walked from the dark of the picnic area toward us, holding hands with the girl Juliet. They came up the steps and Mom stepped aside and held the door open for them. Mom looked across the gap at the dark of the Hudok trailer and she let the door close.

"This is Juliet," said Sister Rae to Mom.

"I know Juliet," Mom said.

"She's going to sleep over," Rae told us.

"If that's okay," Juliet said.

"You'd be doing us a favor," Mom said. "We need ourselves a blond in here."

—

There was popcorn and some talk about how Mom's boss wore the same shoes as Boris Karloff and that night I was the last to go to sleep. It must have been that way before, that I was the one who stayed up longest, but that night was the first night I can remember it, three women under one roof and a little bit of panic in my chest over what my responsibility was, if any.

Boris Karloff wore on to Lon Chaney's Wolf Man and Mom called it a night. She had to open Malley O's brunch next morning. Sister Rae brushed Juliet's hair and they talked for a while about things I half followed until Juliet fell asleep sitting up on the couch. Sister Rae touched her toes to my forehead—I was on the floor—and whispered she was going to bed. She took the girl Juliet by the hand and sleepwalked her back toward the beds, the tall dark head of my sister, the blond girl's hair like a little ghost of its own in the dark of the trailer. I got up onto the couch and pulled the crazy quilt down over me. I could hear Mom say something to Sister Rae and Sister Rae say something back. I listened to my sister brush her teeth and spit and the trailer felt small and definite around me. I would turn thirteen that fall and I would start eighth grade. I didn't know if Sister Rae would go back to finish her senior year or not. I lay there for a while, listening to nothing, until I figured the women were sleeping. I sat up and looked through Mom's purse and I found a secret joint tucked in with her cigarettes. I took her lighter and I opened the door of the trailer and I sat out on the trailer steps, looking out at the world.

It was late but some of our neighbors were still out there, moving around, sitting in their little strips of yard, a lot of cackling and competing music preferences. I didn't know anything about constellations, but they were up there, the sky tamped down, black and low over the trees, a lid through which you could almost see it all.

GRANT PROPOSAL

With your time and money, I'll produce a clone of myself. Then said clone and I will watch tv as the weather guy sends it back to the anchorwoman. *Back to you, Becky*, the weather guy will say, but the camera will stay on him, apparently no one left in the newsroom, no one left in the castle. It's the same with time machines. At some point, you're tempted to go back and kill early family members or trick better-looking people into mating with your early family members, so that instead of you being born it would be an angel who vaguely would have reminded people of you. One school of thought says the metaphor is the body of the ghost. I'm going to spend your grant money looking into this. My clone talks too much, so I'll also need to produce a second clone, the first clone to make love to, of course, and the second clone to go around town, denying it, for I fear the villagers, their quaint beliefs. Yet how I'd like to be invited to their homes! The potted plants. The window treatment. The family lens for spotting ghosts through. A third clone would defend me from the villagers, would be schooled in security, all manner of martial defense. What with his healthful body, I'll have to make sure the other clones don't fall in love with him. So I'll need to purchase cameras to keep track of what's going on in the bedrooms. Soon, though, the four of us will get bored, practicing karate on the lawn, no one to look at but each other. So if there's any money left over, I'd like to hire someone to bring me the brain of the television anchorwoman, kept alive in a glass jar. *I'm just a scientist*, I'll say to it. *Won't you teach me how to dance?*

DEATH TO THE DAYLIGHT PEOPLE

Dear Harold and Sam:

The feet of the daylight people squeak in their shoes and their faces are round and white like paper plates and you shoot one daylight person and three more pop up, each one cleaner than the first. There must be no end to them. They must wash each other's backs and feet by lanternlight. When the wind blows across the river, from their side to ours, it smells like soap. (I do not want to guess what it smells like to the daylight people when the wind blows the other way.) I'm not sure if the daylight people are born. I only know they die when I empty my gun—oompah!—over the hummock. The daylight people will not cease until we're all bathed and powdered and ready for bed. I imagine the oils and the towels. I imagine the bodies of their mothers soaking long and hot in tubs. Even the flame from the barrels of their karen-guns, when they kill us from across the river, looks clean and shapely, little teardrops of happiness. Even the dirty songs they sing in the evening around their campfires—we can hear their sweet voices filter down from the bluffs—exude a nice athletic sexuality one could not begin to dream of, not on this side of the river, where one half of you gets it from the gutter while the other half of you gets it from the back seat of a truck, simultaneously, and you're lucky if you get paid. You know what I'm talking about, the things that go on over here, the things we're fighting for. It's hard to write songs about it, hard to find rhymes. It's hard to be a bringer of death under such conditions.

—

It was hard to be a bringer of death under such conditions, the bridge, the river, the daylight people across it, the sun rising behind. At night the daylight people edged their witches in close to the line, to bring on sleep in us, to lay the daylight curses in you, like so many eggs. Dear Harold and Sam: these were witches in white cloth wraps like grandmas and I'd say one witch installed for every hundred yards of line, each witch aimed at us from the bluffs, spider hands upraised, their longish thumbs almost like an extra finger. They had the high position, from which to blast down their signal with their organized minds. Our guns would not reach them. They seemed to intuit exactly, these witches, how far our guns could reach. I really wanted to shoot a daywitch, just once. I wanted to be known as witch killer, like my bestie, White-Out. Dear Harold and Sam: you know who White-Out is, you knew her before I did. White-Out did not fear a witch, not like me. I feared a witch but at the same time I wanted a witch to float over the river to me, feed me cereal and touch my face, take me away from it all. We were all exhausted, anyway, from being up the night before. We didn't like bedtime. To prevent our succumbing to the witch signal flooding the air lanes, the line bosses would crawl along behind the hummocks in the night, giving us the propaganda the best they could, handing out wasp leaves for us to chew against the invisible narcotic of witch vision. Succumbing was a big problem. The daylight people positioned spotters across the bridge, keeping lookout for those of us nodding off to the witch signal, then sent a swimmer across the river, to cut your throat or open a porthole in your face with one of their shoosh-guns, then disappear from whence they came. It really messed with morale. The wasp leaves worked for a while but sooner or later a body needs sleep, even the filthiest of us. You were left with thistles in your gums and craving more wasp leaves, that's about it. I, for one, always succumbed to witch vision, no matter how many leaves I chewed. I didn't expect to live very long. I just knew I would wake up with a porthole in my face. Each night I was always one of the first to sleep, no matter how I tried. My left foot would twitch, I'd yelp, the taste of witch signal in my nose, fake peach and soap. Then the daylight people would storm the bridge, their faces like hundreds of little white suns, my bestie White-Out jabbing me in the side with her pistolette, saying how the poets lied about sleep, saying how sleep is not at all like death, saying only death is like death, saying wake up and die motherfucker.

—

During the day you'd see carp and buffalo fish nosing the river's surface, sometimes, the V wake of their tails in the shallows. I liked their solidness and girth, these big fish, the weirdness of their soft mouths, too much like ours. A guy in our unit from Carolton—his name was Highlight because of his hair—sometimes saved back toasted white bread, after chow time, to bait the carp, boredom mainly, waiting for the daylight people to finally come kill us. Highlight and some of the other guys would toss the bread out, over the hummock where we formed our line, upstream a little bit to account for the current. When the carp rose for the bread, Highlight and Crewshutter and some of the other guys would pop off small-arms fire at the fish. You don't think about it with fish, but they bleed, those big carp and buffalo have a lot of blood in them. The daylight people, on the other side of the river, would boo whenever a fish got shot. They didn't kill fish over there. I hated to see it myself. It didn't fill me with camaraderie, big carp with its scales made out of gold, its body torn open, only its swim bladder keeping it afloat, little pale balloon in the sunlight for the first and last time, Highlight blowing over his pistol barrel like he was from the Wild West. Most of what I saw and tried to love, other than the bestie White-Out, was nonsense. I guess we had language and small tools and things like that, okay. But even after Death got added to the garden, the difference between man and fish—as far as I could tell—was zero.

—

Nights were the worst, the witches in the bluffs. The witch vision picked away at you, little doubts, failures of masculinity. You'd fall asleep so hard your fingernails would grow at mushroom rate. Even your teeth felt longer. Then the daylight people would storm the bridge, etc. If you were even awake you'd have to kill them with the witch vision superimposed over your slaughter, confusing it, firing your weapon both through and at your dreams. The witches of the daylight people were too high class and subtle to send you nightmares, nothing obvious or over the top like killing your own mother or biting into a small child, the kind of dream where—when you woke up—you'd suss out the vision as an imposition of witchery, say to yourself, That wasn't me, that was a dream. No, these were dreams that worked at you all the next day, unsussable. You thought they were your fault, these dreams, one where I looked down at a crossroads and my penis had two heads, for example, one head pointing to the left and one pointing to the right, the sum total of the dream being me standing there not knowing which direction to go, to the left or to the right, wishing there were a third head, a third direction, that indecision staying with me through my waking day, the kind of thing you might dream, yourself, even if a witch was not involved. That was the genius of it. Or the dream where I was holding hands with my bestie White-Out in a mansion with many rooms. In the dream the bestie White-Out said, "Hey, there's another room over there," and we'd walk into that room, and in that room would be my bestie, White-Out, with whom I thought I was holding hands. In the dream I'd look down at my hand but no one was holding it. I'd have to walk into the room alone. I'd walk over to the new White-Out, the one who'd been in the room already, and she'd stand up and say to me, "Hey, there's another room over there," and I'd say, "No, I want to stay in this room with you," and she'd say, "Come on, let's go," and I'd hold hands with her, walk into this other room, and there she'd be, already sitting in that room, and I'd look down at my hand, again, but no one was holding it.

—

One night, early in my days as a killer of daylight people, back when I didn't know anything and anyone, back before the bestie White Out, the line boss DC came crawling down the line with wasp leaves in his pockets, the moon up above like a garden light, the soft sounds of daylight people singing across the river. We were all jostled and dirty and packed into the mud hummocks like sand fleas. There was a rumor going up and down the line the daylight people would try to push for the bridge that night, etc. They were putting their witches in position, smoke floating over the river, the smell of lather. No one knew what kept the daylight people from taking the bridge, or why they hadn't already. The daylight people were stronger than us and there were more of them and they had better clothes and hairstyles. It was said that they did not mean to take the bridge at all, that the army of daylight people across the river from us were just keeping us occupied while the main offensive against our lives and liberties took place elsewhere. I didn't know what I believed. I looked to the line boss for direction. The line boss DC was a handsome man with a head well shaped like sculpture and he came down the line that night, saying, "Gentlemen, it's not about death to banker's hours. It's not about keeping our homes free from washtubs. It's not economics and it's not about country. Look to your left, look to your right, look at each other. You're fighting for the man next to you." And I did what he said, for he was the line boss. I looked to my right and I saw a dead man, a porthole where his face had been, shooshed out the night previous. I looked to my left down the hummock and saw Tall John, a former stripper with white teeth that glowed in the dark, Tall John being the one who started everyone calling me the Blowjob King. I didn't want to fight for the likes of Tall John, nor for the dead man either, whose name I didn't learn. I understood to be a good killer I would have to find a bestie. Then position myself next to that bestie on the line. Then look to my right or my left and see that bestie. And then have something to murder for.

—

My unit was the Heart Pigs and we were useless as a unit (oom-pah!) and our line boss was the man DC. DC was a known coward, well liked by the Heart Pigs for keeping us alive instead of murdered by daylight people, for he talked a good game but would not take risks with us or himself, not like the line boss of the Meeming Screamies, who volunteered his boys for every mission. Our DC was a graying exhausted man with a face that belonged on ancient coins and it was his good looks and kind eyes that had gotten him so far up the chain of command, that and how DC was one of the few of us impervious to witch signal. DC would say of the witches, "Witches are ladies and ladies do not charm me." DC would pat us on the heads and pull us back from the line for R and R whenever he could, handing out pills for us to use on R and R so that we would feel loved by him when we weren't around him, love in the blood, love in the blood, DC said, keeping one or two of his favorite Heart Pigs with him in his hotel room at the commandeered Motel 6. It wasn't that DC played favorites, he just had favorites. I was not one of his favorites, but still DC was kind to me. Like I said, I was new to the unit, fresh from the farm, too wide across the shoulders and milk-fed to be a favorite of the line boss DC. DC told me he preferred a skinny soldier for his favorites. He told me in his tent, "Come back when you've lost a little weight." He said, "I like the sense of a certain privation." So, until I got skinny enough, or otherwise figured out what the word "privation" was, instead I'd go drinking and whoring with the other unselected Heart Pigs, in a tavern on Wabash Avenue called the Birdhouse, back from the line about a mile from the bridge, where the witch signal could not trouble our merriment.

—

But this is a story about White-Out, above all. Dear Harold and Sam: how I'd come to be White-Out's sidekick is: I helped her write a letter to one of her boyfriends for her. It is not news to you, Harold and Sam, that White-Out had boyfriends. This was at the tavern called the Birdhouse. Amongst the Heart Pigs the girl White-Out was respected as killer of the enemy and even known as dangerous to friends if you got on her wrong side, the best shot in the unit, a deadeye across the river, a little weird even for a girl, a little too into singing songs to herself, the only one of us who had ever killed a daywitch, a witch who'd floated down too close to the river to take a piss in the night, her witch face exploding into dandelion seeds as she squatted, finding her way into—but not out of—White-Out's sights. White-Out was very tall and I liked her blond hair and gray eyes and she carried with her, in addition to the karen-gun we all carried, a long gun with a scope. She kept it strapped across her broad back. The line boss DC liked to send White Out to the rooftops just back from the line, to put a damper on the daylight people from above. White Out's gun had the longest reach in the unit, probably in the whole battalion. White-Out kept to herself and had never said a word to me. And though she was respected, no one really seemed to like White-Out, or at least everyone kept their distance from her, due to how White-Out was a girl, of course, and at the same time taller than any of us, and also the size of her skull, which was a monument, plus due to how White-Out had cut off the pinky finger of the Heart Pig morale officer, a guy everyone called Lucky Daryl. Lucky Daryl had made a comment about White-Out's forehead being the size of a drive-in movie screen. And then Lucky Daryl had nine fingers. You didn't want to fuck with White Out.

—

But what did I know? She was sitting alone in a back booth, a battered pencil in her hand, writing, a look of concentration upon her face, no one in the Birdhouse but soldiers off the line and locals there to fleece them. I'd been sitting with Tall John and some of the other Heart Pigs, Crewshutter and Lucky Daryl, Die Curious and Red Delicious, other people I didn't really like but wanted to like me. They'd each been talking of their girlfriends back home and how far they'd gotten with them sexually. I was dreading this conversation because, at the time, I had no girlfriend back home.

So, before it became my turn to lie, I stood up with my very tall beer can and worked my way through the dancing boys and girls, hired entertainment at the Birdhouse, toward the booth where White-Out was sitting, my facial expression saying to the Heart Pigs, "Fuck you guys anyway." When Tall John and the other Heart Pigs got the sense of where I was headed, you could hear them hooting and hissing behind me, saying how the Blowjob King had himself a love interest, saying White-Out was so tall I better find a step stool if I was going to get it on. I sat down in the booth across from White-Out and I tried to pretend I didn't know we were being hooted at. White-Out's forehead was large, yes, but something about the expanse of it comforted me. And I said to her immediately, for I wanted a bestie, "I think you're trustworthy and brave."

—

The girl White-Out raised her eyes and got a look at me. Her gray eyes were as big as her hands. She said, "You're the one everyone calls the Blowjob King."

"I don't know about everyone," I said.

She said, "How many blowjobs before they king you?"

"One," I said.

"One?" she said.

"Three," I said.

—

Her face was a large face and her ears too small for it. Dear Harold and Sam: I thought she looked lovely, even with the soot and charcoal she rubbed into her face and forehead, you know, to keep herself from being an easy target on the line. The forehead was large and my guess was she kept a large brain safe behind it. Rightly she feared that a daylight person, across the river, would see her grand forehead, aim for it. I tried not to stare at the fetching forehead and we drank for a while awkwardly and we talked of small things, our points of origin, how neither of us had ever owned a pet, how we both had herpes but neither of us had ever voted. You could hear the nucka-nuck of small-arms fire from the line, plus the sound of a poorly planned parade in the streets outside the Birdhouse, a march out there played on what sounded like pots and pans. Across the bar floor the other Heart Pigs started picking out their prostitutes, boy ones and girl ones, sun ones, moon ones, then disappeared into the upstairs rooms. White-Out asked me if I would be contracting with a prostitute and I told her that I had thought about it carefully but had finally decided not to. Then White-Out surprised me by putting her boots into my lap—size twelve—and talking to me about the letter she was writing to her boyfriend, a pacifist who'd stayed on the farm back in Floyd's Knobs. She seemed to love this boyfriend very much.

"I think he's secretly a day person," White-Out said, almost shyly. She took her boots from my lap and stood and came around the booth and sat down next to me. She put her hand on my knee. "In his heart, I mean," White-Out said. "Only he doesn't want to tell me. He likes trees. He likes windmills."

"There are a lot of people like that," I said. I scooted down to give White-Out room on the seat. She scooted down along with me to stay close. I scooted a little more, till I was touching the wall with my shoulder. She scooted close again, so she had me pinned against the wall. She took my hand in hers.

"But I love him," White-Out said. She pressed my hand as if she were counting the bones in it. This friendship was moving fast. She held up the cocktail napkin upon which she'd been writing. "I want to tell him how much I miss him. But when I write that down, it just seems dumb."

"What do you miss about him?" I asked her.

She thought. She said, "I miss how he doesn't care how tall I am. I miss how he doesn't cry when he comes, which is something I can't say about boys around here."

I said, "That's beautiful. Just write it down."

She wrote it down. She looked at what she'd written. She looked sideways at me and she smiled.

—

Then White-Out told me she could tell the difference between daywitches, that each witch had a certain flavor of dream they'd send you, like a signature.

"I didn't know there was a difference between witches," I said.

"The two witches nearest the bridge are the strongest witches," White-Out said. She put her arm around my shoulders. She unbuttoned the first two buttons of my shirt and slipped her hand inside. Her body pressed me against the bar wall. I felt small, portable. She pinched my nipple and she said, "I call these witches the twins. One sends you dreams that taste like vegetables. The other sends you dreams that feel all furry."

"No one's ever pinched my nipple before," I said to White-Out.

"You seem okay with it," White-Out said.

"And I never noticed this thing, about vegetables and fur, when it comes to witch signal," I said.

"You'll notice it now," she said.

"I will pay more attention."

"Do your pants zip or button?" she asked.

"You have a boyfriend," I said.

"And don't you forget it," White-Out said.

—

You need to get yourself a war friend. Your life changes for the better and you learn a lot of things about the world. One of the first improvements was that White-Out arranged it so that I would no longer give blowjobs for free. One day she gathered up the other Heart Pigs in a semicircle near the cookfires, back from the line a bit, on the football field of the old college, the bluffs of the daylight people just visible beyond her high shoulders. There was the male cook Jezebel and the female cook Earnwright. There was Tall John and Lucky Daryl. The weird kid with the inverted tooth, Max. There were the line boss DC's two current favorite Heart Pigs, the lithe blond named Hazel and the lithe blond named Guildenstern. There were a couple of other fellows from some of the other units, the Karate Kids and the Meeming Screamies. White-Out stood taller than any of them, unloved but highly respected, which I decided was a kind of love. Her karen-gun looked small like a toy gun strapped across her middle. She lifted her large palms outward and said, "The Blowjob King is no longer a given. How long did you think you could go without paying your respects?"

The fellows all grumbled to hear this. Crewshutter spat, not at me, but in my direction. Tall John kicked at a ball of mud and raised his hand. White-Out pointed at him. Tall John said, "I'm the one who named him the Blowjob King. I should get a discount."

"No discounts," White-Out said.

—

I learned White-Out loved the pacifist boyfriend in Floyd's Knobs very much. I learned also that the boyfriend in Floyd's Knobs was not her only boyfriend. White-Out had boyfriends in six different cities and she was, as you well know, married to two men. White-Out told me how these two men, her husbands, Harold and Sam were their names, lived together on a chicken farm in New Harmony. They counted eggs and waited patiently for White-Out's return, for she was wife to them both and beloved, chicken plucker and head of household, the one who passed out the dinner rolls. White-Out told me when the fight against the daylight people was over and we were still alive she would take me to the farm in New Harmony and introduce me to Harold and Sam. "Then we'll see how it goes from there," White-Out said, taking her boots off, putting her feet in my lap. We were best friends in the bar, in the streets, on the line. For White-Out, I decided, I would fight a war against god if I had to.

—

One night on the line I said this same exact thing to White-Out. White-Out said, "It's like we're fighting a war against god already, or hadn't you realized that?"

I said, "How so?"

She pointed across the river. I curled up next to her like a plant. She slipped her hand inside my shirt. I could hear Tall John snickering down the line, whispering I was pussy-whipped, but I didn't care. I could see his dumb face white in the dark down the mud line and I stuck my tongue out at it. White-Out said, "Over there, on that side of the river, the daylight people: they are clean. They bathe each evening. They stand facing each other and they throw balls back and forth in a game of catch. They have projects. They are fruitful. They don't laugh at each other when they are naked. They're the forces of the day. We're the forces of the night."

"I've never thought of it that way," I said.

"It's that way," she said.

"Against god," I said.

"Yes," she said.

"I don't like our chances," I said.

"We have no chance," she said. I pushed my bootheels into the mud so I could get myself closer to White-Out. She let me push against her. She asked, "How many blowjobs did you give today?"

I said, "One."

"One?" she asked.

"Three," I said.

—

White-Out was good across the river with the pistolette and karen-gun, but her great pleasure was the sniper rifle. The gun was long and oiled and White-Out named the gun after her father, Clarence. She loved her father, Clarence, who was dead. She loved her many boyfriends and her two husbands, Harold and Sam, and she dictated to me correspondence with these men. I wrote to them all for her. On R and R at the Birdhouse, in our little booth, with the nucka-nuck of small-arms fire coming from the river, White-Out would say to me, out loud, "Dear Paul, you have steady hands and you are not frightened of me when I move around in the dark," and I would write that down for her. White-Out would say, "Dear Clancy, I met a guy who reminds me a lot of you and I slept with him," and I would write this down for her. White-Out would say, "Dear Eric, I'm in love with you just as much as I'm in love with your sister."

"Sister?" I would say.

"Sister," White-Out would say, and I would write it down for her.

—

With the blowjob money I made, White-Out would go to the temporary PX and buy pink cigarettes and cream-filled cakes and a pint or two of the yellow liquor they called benzene. When the line boss DC would send White-Out to the rooftops with her sniper rifle, she'd take me along with her to watch her back and check her feet for sore spots. Down from the hummock line and the bridge we'd go together, back down Wabash Avenue a few blocks, saying hidey-do to the local citizenry, through the fluctuating doors and into the abandoned lobby of the old-timey hotel, with its ancient "Free Cable" sign and empty candy jar, up the long emergency staircase, fifteen floors to the rooftop level, where we'd spread out a little blanket and have a picnic in the sun, just the two of us, eating and drinking while White-Out plinked at daylight people with the sniper rifle named Clarence. The hotel overlooked the downtown area, positioned nicely to give White-Out a shot off either side of the bridge. The hotel rooftop was easily my favorite part of the war, getting drunk on blowjob money, checking White-Out's feet for sore spots, far from the other Heart Pigs and their night-boy games. Her boots didn't fit her large feet right and it always hurt her feet to come up all those emergency stairs. The heaviness of her bare foot in my hand made me thankful, though seeing the actual soles of her feet troubled me in a heartsick way. Feet are meant to be connected to the ground, is my way of looking at it. When you see the bottom of a person's foot, there's something almost too vulnerable about it. Death comes sneaking around. You only see a foot like that when you are lucky, and then you have to question your luck. And I sometimes grew sad to have such a friend as White-Out, her feet in my hands while she pulled Clarence's trigger. So many people had to die in order for my happiness to work its way through history to find me. And who was I? It's like the whole war had been invented to put me on a rooftop with my bestie, the sun out like a voyeur, soaking all my happiness up second-hand.

—

I mentioned this to her, up on the rooftops one day, how the war had been invented for us to find each other. White-Out said to me, simply, "You're right about that." I was scanning the bluffs with binoculars while White-Out scanned the bluffs with Clarence's scope. The bluffs from that distance looked made of chalkboard material. It was the bluffs on the far side of the river, the bridge, the hummocks on our side of the river, Wabash Avenue leading from the bridge and right to the foot of the hotel. Behind us was the park and the women's cemetery. In front of us, in between the hotel and the bridge, the downtown area lay stretched out beneath, like a plan. From that high perspective I could tell how thought had gone into the layout of the town, whenever they'd built it, the patterning of the grid, which I never thought about when I was down in the streets, where everything seemed improvisational, where streets seemed to exist because I turned and walked down them. Up on the roof the breeze blew oddly, bouncing all around you like a dog. It was my job to think about the wind, to look for day faces on the leftward side of the bridge. White-Out unwrapped a cream-filled cake and bit into it. I said to White-Out, "You see that little shrub, just down from the water pump?"

She set half of the cream-filled cake on the rooftop ledge and shouldered Clarence and scanned, the weird breeze fondling her blond hair. "Check," White-Out said.

"You see how there's a guy hiding behind it?"

"Check," White-Out said.

—

Clarence bucked against White-Out's shoulder and we watched the face of the daylight person behind the shrub turn into a dandelion puff and blow away on the breeze. I rested my binoculars on my chest and leaned my back against the rooftop ledge and looked up at the sun. I liked the heavy pull of the cord around my neck with the binoculars hanging from it. I could feel a straight line drawn from the weight of the binoculars, down fifteen stories, right to the center of the Earth, which is where we were all headed.

"You say I'm right about it?" I asked her.

"About what?" she said. She put her back to the ledge and lit a pink cigarette. There was a little dollop of cream on her upper lip and I watched the triangle of her tongue find it.

I said, "How the war was invented to put me on the rooftop with my bestie White-Out."

White-Out said, "You've got that right. Only," she said, "you're wrong to be sad about it." She blew out a cloud of pink smoke and she passed me the cigarette.

"All these people had to die," I said.

"Yes," she said. She said it like she'd bitten the word off of a larger word. I didn't want her to be angry with me. She said, "A long time ago, your mother gave birth to you." She picked up the cream-filled cake from the ledge and put it in her mouth. She asked me to show her my bellybutton. I lifted my shirt and showed her. She put her finger in my bellybutton. She left a trace of cream filling there. "Then there was a war. I walked a long way to find it. You walked a long way to find it."

"I didn't mean to upset you," I said.
"Go sit on the other side of the rooftop for a while," she said.

—

Another day, same rooftop, more blowjob money.
"When did you know you were a night person?" White-Out asked me.
I'd been worried about this question. I wasn't sure I was, truly, a night person. I tried to answer truthfully. "Before I met you," I said, "I did prefer nighttime. I preferred having dreams to being awake. I preferred dinner to breakfast. It was all very clear."
She squeezed off a shot and I lifted my binoculars in time to watch a daylight person fall from the bridge into the river.
"And now that you've met me?"
"Well," I said. "I know it's not right. But I think about the sunshine more often. I think I could enjoy a hammock. I think I might like to go to a beach."
"Don't talk that kind of talk to anyone but me," she said.

—

In a way, though, I thought the line boss DC would be proud of us. We had found a friend to be honest with. As long as we killed day people, we didn't have to be patriotic.
"Do you think they pay for sex on the other side?" I asked White-Out.
"No," she said. "If anything, they exchange goods and services."
I thought about that. "I'm happy to be where I am," I said to White-Out.
"I'm happy too," she said. She said, "You know what I like to do when I'm happy?"
"I do," I said. I lay down on the blanket, the gravel of the rooftop pressing up through the cloth of it. I unbuttoned my jeans so that White-Out could watch me masturbate. There was a war going on. My masturbation was something she liked to see. She said it made her brainwaves flatten out. She said how when she watched

me she liked to think about those people in the world who look past death and choose life. She took a swig of the yellow liquor while she watched me, the sun up behind her large head, like her blond twin. I settled in to my position. She ate a cream-filled cake. Her eyes were gray, like soft rocks. The breeze blew through her hair and toward me. She smelled like sweat and tobacco. And when I was done, she flipped a coin of blowjob money onto my stomach, as a reward.

She said, "That was real peaceful. Thank you."

—

That last night we were back on the line with the other Heart Pigs, dusk, the daylight people moving their witches up. I no longer bothered to space myself out on the line like we were supposed to. I placed myself directly next to White-Out, right at arm's length. The vegetable witch was up and sending signal and there was a new witch to contend with. Or so White-Out said. She could feel a new witch over there, a powerful new vibration. White-Out was trying to get a feel for the signature, her big eyes closed. Her eyelids had more surface area than most eyelids, like pink lawns. Tall John and the Heart Pig they called Dr. Marfan had nicked a roll of measuring tape from a wrecked tailor's shop on Third Street. To kill time, the Heart Pigs were giving themselves hard-ons and measuring, tossing the tape down the line to the next guy. Dr. Marfan and Tall John had been surprised to discover their penises were the exact same length and girth, down to the eighth. They guffawed and proclaimed themselves dick twins and gave each other air high-fives. Tall John's sidekick Crewshutter measured out larger, but he looked glum in the face about it. Crewshutter couldn't be dick twins with his bestie, which was what he most wanted. He was jealous of Dr. Marfan. I myself didn't want to do this night-boy game of measuring penises and I knew I wouldn't have to because I was sitting next to White-Out. The Heart Pigs wouldn't think of tossing the measuring tape in her direction. In the middle of this White-Out opened her eyes and said to me, "Elements."

I said, "What?"

She closed her eyes again. You could see the white robe and upstretched hands of the new witch, across the river, up in the bluffs. To me she looked like all the other witches, but I trusted White-Out's sense of things. "Elements," White-Out said. "Air and fire, I think."

—

I closed my eyes, to see if I could suss the new witch. But before I could, one of the line boss DC's favorites, the lithe blond Guildenstern, came crawling up to us through the mud. He was a beautiful boy and he had a tattoo on the back of his hand with a heart that said "Rosenbloom," a friend of his who'd had his face shooshed out during the early days of the stand on the river. He stayed low in his crawl and he tapped one of White-Out's large boots. He wasn't happy about having to crawl through the mud, but what could you tell him about it? We were night people. A certain amount of filth was to be expected. Guildenstern made a face at White-Out and he said, "DC wants to see you."

—

The field headquarters of the line boss DC was a three-man tent set back from the line, dead center in the home endzone of the old college football field. It was a small tent but DC had it kitted out nicely, a lot of red velvet and blanketry, a hookah and a solar-powered lava lamp, an LED disco ball, a couple of plastic ferns placed outside, stolen from the waiting room of a doctor's office. You had to sit in the mud at the mouth of the small tent to meet with DC. White-Out and I sat down and Guildenstern opened the tent flap. DC was sitting inside with the other lithe blond, Hazel, playing a card game. Hazel and Guildenstern said hello to each other and Guildenstern strolled off toward the cookfires over at the fifty-yard line. In the tent DC smoked a small knotty-looking cigar and its smoke filled the tent and smelled like grapes.

"End of the line," DC said. There was a half-inch of ash on his cigar and he leaned across and tapped his ash into Hazel's shirt pocket.

"End of the line, sir?" White-Out said.

DC nodded and played a card. Hazel looked at the card and said, "Fuck." DC's handsomeness was broad and comforting and you could see he would win the card game. He lay his cards face down and turned and looked at us. He said, "You boys are some of my best boys. Even though one of you is a lady and ladies do not charm me."

"You don't have to say that every time we talk," said White-Out.

"In short," DC said, "I called you here to tell you we're going to be defeated tonight."

I looked at White-Out but she didn't look at me. "How do you know?" White-Out asked.

The lithe blond Hazel chuckled as if this were a dumb question. He patted at his shirt pocket to make sure DC's cigar ash didn't catch him on fire. DC shushed Hazel and pulled a piece of paper from a stack of them and held it out toward White-Out. White-Out read the piece of paper and she handed it to me. It was a message from the day people. The paper was a thick and fine paper and it smelled like lilacs. The note read, "It's been fun, but we will defeat you tonight. Signed, the day people." I handed the piece of paper back to DC. "They have very high-quality paper," DC said. He sniffed at the note and touched his tongue to it.

"Nothing but the best," Hazel said meanly.

"I thought I felt some weird mojo on the line," White-Out said of the note.

"Mojo," Hazel said.

"Yeah," DC said, cutting his hand in the air. "As a deal," he said, "it's all done."

White-Out and I sat there looking at Hazel and DC. Hazel and DC sat there looking back. When it was clear there was nothing else to be said, they started playing cards again.

"Oompah," White-Out said.

—

With the last of the blowjob money White-Out bought some cream-filled cakes and a bottle of the yellow liquor they called benzene. At a drugstore she bought some hair ties with jeweled butterflies on them and she bought some lick-on tattoos and she bought a pack of pink cigarettes. And we took Clarence and the other guns with us. And we packed some extra ammo and a couple of grenades into the picnic basket. And we walked the fifteen stories up to the rooftop of the old-timey hotel, where we'd make our last stand. It was night and at that distance you could just feel the little flippery edge of the witch signal. We stood on the ledge, both breathing hard from the emergency stairs. We looked over the city to the river. Among the bluffs and tree line on the far side of the river there were amassing so many daylight people that, with their clean skin and hair, they looked like false dawn, a glow in the teeth of the bluffs like they were a sun rising directly out of a huge mouth. White-Out took my hand in hers. The doglike wind played White-Out's fine blond hair this way and that. She said, "When they come at dawn, I'll shoot as many as I can. They'll come across the bridge," she said, pointing at the bridge, there like a small lit tongue saying "ah" over the river, "and then they'll come over the hummocks. I'll shoot them on the hummocks. Then they'll come down the street. I'll shoot them in the street. By that time," she said, "they'll know where we are, and they'll come up for us. What you'll do," she said, pointing at the cross streets just below us, "is watch for them to get that far. When they get that far," she said, stepping back off the ledge and sitting down on the blanket, "you'll take your karen-gun and my pistolette and you'll kill them when they come up the stairway."

"I understand," I said.

"And when I hear you're in trouble," she said, "I'll come to you."

—

I sat down on the blanket next to her. "We could just leave," I said, though I knew it wasn't possible.

"It isn't possible," White-Out said. "This is part of it."

"This is part of it," I said.

She squeezed my hand and asked me to take my shirt off. I took my shirt off. She put her hair up with one of the butterfly hair ties and she used a second butterfly to put my hair up with. She selected a heart-shaped tattoo from the lick-on book she'd bought and she tore out the paper and she leaned down and licked the heart-shaped tattoo onto me, over my heart. She pulled back the thin paper and the tattoo heart was blue and blurry. "No jerking off tonight," she said. "We need to keep our teeth sharp."

—

Toward dawn White-Out said, out loud, "Dear Harold and Sam." She was scanning the bridge with her scope. She settled and breathed and pulled Clarence's trigger and her shoulder bucked. I got the notebook and pencil from our picnic basket and I started my dictation. "Dear Harold and Sam," I said. White-Out nodded. "I miss you both very much," White-Out said, shucking the spent shell, scanning again. "I think about our home on the farm. I miss being in the small bed with you, Harold. And I miss being in the small bed with you, Sam. And I miss being in the big bed, on Sunday night, with both of you. And I hope it doesn't hurt your feelings to hear this," she said, leaning Clarence on the ledge and turning toward me, "but often, in the dark, in the big bed, when we are all three in it together, I cannot tell the difference between the two of you."

—

Like a dream it happened just as White-Out said. White-Out shot them as they came across the bridge at dawn, their very armpits glowing clean in the dawn light, the overpowering smell of lilac and honey, knots of their bodies, the shine of their smiling teeth as they came across the bridge. My own teeth went slick and electrified. White-Out shot daylight people in the river, where they swam carelessly with their shoosh-guns held between their lips. I watched what I could through the binoculars. "Seven," White-Out said. She pulled Clarence's trigger. "Eight," White-Out said. I put a grenade in my pocket and I took White-Out's pistolette from her waistband, the metal of it hot from her body. From that distance the war sounded like a sporting event, a dull and slushy roar of voices. I watched the section of line guarded by our fellow Heart Pigs. I couldn't tell one Heart Pig from another but I could see how they weren't going to be Heart Pigs for much longer. There were just too many daylight people. In my mind I said goodbye to Tall John and the rest of them, people I didn't care about, but still I felt bad, even guilty. They were dead now or dying and I still had minutes left to live, watching White-Out be White-Out, the sun making her hair white. I was running on religious time, miracle time. The day people overran the football field and they came down Wabash Avenue now, slipping into the street, the pure white of their pajamas, their bright white sneakers, shooting the Heart Pigs and the Karate Kids and the Hoosier Daddys who fled before them, the local citizenry tossing flowers and candy at them as they came. "Twenty-one," said White-Out. "Twenty-two," she said. You could see their faces now, in the street below, smiling, white teeth well brushed for a lifetime. A clutch of daylight people stood in the middle of the cross street beneath us, looking this way and that, their guns at their sides, smoke blowing down the street, the cheers of local citizenry. White-Out said, "Here we go," and she shot into the clutch of daylight people in the cross street below. I watched a face turn into a puff of dandelion seed and blow off down the street. One of the remaining day people watched his friend fall and then looked up. It was a male. He smiled at us and pointed. "Get to the stairs," White-Out said.

—

"Get to the stairs," White-Out says. And I cross the gravel rooftop and open the emergency door. I stand at the top of the stairs, White-Out and the open world behind me. I can hear the feet of the daylight people in the stairwell below, squeaking cleanly in their clean shoes. It's the nibbling, cheerful sound of doom. The dread smell of lilacs floats up the staircase and I redo my hair in the butterfly hair tie and I kiss my palm and touch it to the blurry blue heart tattoo on my chest. I can hear the daylight people jostling up the stairwell now, the sound of their guns clinking together like champagne glasses. In my hand the pistolette is still warm from White-Out's body. And I crouch at the top of the stair and cock the pistolette, which turns it into a living thing, and in my mind I write a letter, to you, Harold and Sam, househusbands of the bestie, White-Out. "Dear Harold and Sam, they call me the Blowjob King. I've seen the bottoms of White-Out's feet and I find them considerable. I have lived on a farm in my life and I know a thing or two about chickens. I will love what you love and this will make us brothers."

ONE MUST FIRST ESTABLISH A RELATIONSHIP WITH THE READER

1

Dear Reader, you seem to not have shaved anything, anything at all. You walk around out there, thinking you're not trapped in a box. When you think you're being stealthy you sound a little bit like a marching band thrown down the stairs. When is the expiration date of your eyes always on me? Again and again I am placed in the holy light of calendars. Couldn't you look at anything else? When was the last time your feet did not touch the ground because your father lifted you? Don't act like you love me. Don't act like you had a father.

2

Dear Reader, if you like plot it means you are afraid to die. Sometimes I lie and say to you that I have never read a book that I have, in fact, read. And this is because I know there's a good chance, thinking that I have not read that book, that you will read that book to me, aloud, for my edification, all night long.

3

Dear Reader, whenever you read to me, in my mind I put on the smallest dress. I do not want to die wearing this fast-food-restaurant t-shirt I'm wearing. Not like my fathers and my father's fathers. The hand jobs, in those days, were never electives. You said to me once that you were sad. We were out in your backyard, watching the bounce house deflate. Once again the birthday party had been planned on the wrong day. So here's my only advice, which works for any situation: close your eyes, like I do, and think about the saints.

4

Dear Reader, when I met you in the forest you were afraid of the forest. Bird feathers clumped around your exit wounds. You and I, so quick, had a baby. We planned a succession of birthday parties for that baby. It was standing over there. God, it even looked like a baby. I tried to hold your hand but, as always, your foot got involved. I was on the wrong side of history. When I said "two peas in a pod" you pretended to think I said "two Petes." It was August, and there wouldn't be anything left to love by September. It was the summer of two Petes, one of whom had your phone number, one of whom has your rain slicker. "When will we ever tell the same lie?" you asked. Come back, dear Reader, you sweet romantic. I am your own true system. I will no longer speak ill of the dead.

THE REGENERATING BOY

The Regenerating Boy: no one knew he was the Regenerating Boy. There was a moon that looked directly at him, and there was a moon that turned its back and hid its face, and often he felt these two moons were the same moon, and the sun did whatever the sun did and he paid it no mind, and no one knew that he was the Regenerating Boy, no one knew, that is, except for his sister, who was his older sister, whose name was Lila.

—

Lila was blond and Lila was tall and she was the scale of things. When the Regenerating Boy looked out at the cornfield and saw the silo he thought: how many Lilas is it high? And when he looked down the road, toward a distant barn or homestead, he thought: how long would it take Lila to walk there?

—

In the farmhouse, there had been a mother and a father, both. The mother and the father, though they lived with their children in the farmhouse, were not farmers. The children weren't sure what their parents were, or did. The mother and the father didn't love Lila and her brother, who was the Regenerating Boy. The parents didn't love their children, though they said they did, and sometimes they even acted like they did.

—

Once, when she and her brother were both smaller, Lila remembered a time. The time was like this: the mother, who was still alive and had not yet been murdered by the father (which would happen, off stage, soon enough), did not like that the little boy, Lila's brother, had hidden his peas in his mashed potatoes.

"I can very well see the peas," said the mother.

"No, you can't," said the Regenerating Boy.

"Don't tell me what I can see," said the mother.

"You can't see anything," said the boy.

"Go to your room," said the father, and the boy stood and walked up the stairs and went to his room, which was also Lila's room, and Lila remembered all of this. She remembered, after finishing her own peas, how she had excused herself from her father (whose beard was twelve different colors) and had excused herself from her mother (who was still alive and had not yet been murdered, off stage, by the father), how she had walked carefully, as a sister, up the stairs, to check on her brother, who was the Regenerating Boy.

—

"They don't love us," said the Regenerating Boy to his sister. "They act like they love us, they tell us they love us, but they don't love us." Lila had opened the door to her brother's room, which was also her room, and her brother had been sitting on the single windowsill of the room, with his back to the window, and the window was open, as was their habit during the heat of the summer, and her brother had said, "They don't love us. They just pretend to."

"I know," she said. She said, "I know they don't love us."

"What am I going to do about it?" he asked.

And Lila hadn't meant to say what she said, she had just been frustrated with her brother, because he did not yet know how to play along with the mother and the father, which made things so much easier in the peeling white farmhouse, to play along with the parents' way of seeing things, and so she said to her brother, "You could always fall out the window backwards and kill yourself."

And that's just what her brother, the Regenerating Boy, did: he smiled at his sister Lila's advice. He tucked into a ball. He fell out of the window backwards like he was going scuba diving.

—

Lila braced herself on the windowsill to look down at her brother, crimped on the dark stumblestones, a small bent shape. His neck looked like a marionette's neck looks. His eyes were open and pointed at the sky and the eyes had nothing but two moons in them, a moon in each of them, and Lila looked up at the sky, also, to see how many moons there were, but there was just the one moon, and she turned out of the room with a feeling of dreadful excitement in her chest and she was on the steps going down and her father and still-living mother were in the living room, not talking to each other, just sitting on the couch, washed in the blue light of the television, and Lila did not say anything to these parents and she turned down the hall and popped open the front door of the farmhouse. What she had meant to do was to rush down the steps of the porch and then be seen cradling her dead brother in her arms by the time her parents figured out what all had happened. But when she opened the door her little brother was standing there, alive, no moons in his eyes, his fist raised to knock on the door, as if he were a visitor to this house, a weird little smile on his face, and his neck looked just fine, and there was nothing at all wrong, and this was the first time Lila suspected that her brother might be the Regenerating Boy.

—

"Do you remember when you fell from the window?" the sister Lila would sometimes, later, ask her brother.

She would ask it as they lay in their bed together. She would ask it when the voices of their parents, below them in the house, rumbled up from the floorboards, like whales beneath an ocean, and how the seasons passed, and how the voices would rise and rise up to Lila and then how, inevitably, the voices of the parents would turn mean and then mean trouble. She asked about the window when she had her arms around her little brother. She asked about the window when she grew afraid and didn't want her brother to know she was afraid.

And her little brother would say, "No." He would say it truthfully, as he was young and wasn't yet making memories very well. "No, I don't remember about the window," he would say, "but please tell me the story."

But Lila wouldn't tell him the story. All she wanted was to know if he remembered it. She would shush him then and breathe in his ear to help him sleep, and she would wait to hear the footsteps of her parents on the stairs. She had seen her brother in the window and then disappear from the window. She had said to him, "Why don't you fall out the window?" and the little boy, her brother, had done it, done what she said, just like that, which was a powerful feeling in her chest. She had looked down and seen the marbles of his eyes looking up at her from the stumblestones, but the eyes of her brother had not been looking at anything. It was all so strange that she wasn't sure it had really happened the way she remembered it, that she truly remembered he was her brother and that he had been dead. How could that have been? How could that have been, when her brother smelled like mint and milk, when her brother twitched in her arms as he fell asleep, when he was in her arms in the bed they shared and warm and very much alive?

—

The second time, though, there could be no doubt that her brother was the Regenerating Boy.

The second time happened after the father had murdered the mother, off stage, and dropped the mother's body in the well behind the house.

And this second time happened after her father had taken her, Lila, barefoot and only in her pajama bottoms, Lila as the eldest child, as the child of some understanding, and marched her down the long path to the well, his twelve-colored beard lighting up the night, down the long path in her bare feet, and he had said to her,

her father had said to her, looking down the mouth of the well into the darkness, "Your mother sent me a letter from California."

"That's not true," Lila said to her father.

"It is true," her father said.

He had said this about California, her father, lying to her about the mother, but showing her the truth of the well, both telling her and not telling her what had happened to the mother. Her father had said, "Your mother," pointing his finger down the darkness of the well, "has gone to California, and she's never coming back."

—

And but this second time, this time after the father had murdered the mother, there could be no doubt that her brother was the Regenerating Boy.

This second time had been during hide-and-seek, a week or so after her father had marched her down the path to the well where her mother—who had gone to California—was buried. Their father, he was not in the house that next day. Where had he been? Lila didn't remember. Maybe in town. Maybe with the male friends and their breath and their cars and their strange talk in the tavern. Maybe holding hands with a woman in the tavern and telling the woman tales about how his wife, who was no good, had fled to California, leaving him and her children behind. Lila wouldn't put anything past this father. And the girl Lila had said to her brother, on that day, alone in the house, "I'll hide, and I'll play the mother, and you'll try to find me."

—

Her brother was small and he went along with what she said without question, and Lila felt, as usual, the power of that, which made her feel taller than she was, which made the muscles of her legs feel strong. He was still small (though not as small as he had once been) and he did what she said about hide-and-seek and his small hands covered his large eyes and he started counting to a hundred. Lila walked out the front door and closed the front door heavily behind her, to make it sound to her brother like she had gone outside to hide, and she walked around the peeling farmhouse, to the back door, which she had, in craft, left open, left open before she had suggested a game of hide-and-seek, before she had said to her brother that she would play the mother and he would need to seek to find her. She walked in through the kitchen and into the living room and looked at her brother, unawares, her brother who played by her rules so well that it made her heart ache. He sat on the couch and his small hands still covered his large eyes and he was counting twenty, twenty-one. She took off her shoes and wiped the bottoms of her two feet and she took the stairs as quietly as she could and went down the hall to her parents' bedroom, where she hid in the closet where her mother had kept her clothes when her mother was alive and still needed clothes. The closet still smelled like her mother, though her mother's clothes were not hanging on the hangers anymore, as her father had carried off large garbage bags full of her mother's clothes and shoes, had driven the bags to the dump. So that the hangers were whatever hangers were when they didn't have clothes hanging on them anymore, and in the closet Lila could smell the lingering leather odor of her mother's shoes, her shoes which were also not in the closet. She could smell her mother's body and her mother's feet. And she waited for what seemed like a long time, waited for her brother to come find her. She waited and she had to pee. She regretted hiding where she had hidden, regretted hiding too well. She regretted, also, that she had fallen asleep.

—

Lila fell asleep and she was having a dream where she stood at the mouth of the well behind the farmhouse and looked down into the darkness of it and felt her father's hand steady on her bare shoulder. She looked down and she saw her mother's eyes open like gems in the darkness and there were two moons in those eyes and she wished her mother, down there, would say something up to her, which is when she felt foolish because she understood, even in the dream, that her mother no longer had a mouth, let alone eyes, and was not in California. Which is when of course her dream was interrupted by her brother, who was the Regenerating Boy. Her brother pulled open the door of the mother's closet, tears in his eyes, and said to Lila, "You're the mother and I found you."

—

She had been angry at her brother for interrupting her dream, which was a dream in which she felt like she was having—even as sad as it was—some interaction with her mother, who had not been a loving mother, who was no longer alive. She had leapt up for the knob of the door and told her brother he was unwanted and she yanked the door closed on him, forgetting the game of hide-and-seek altogether, and it was only when the door bounced back unshut that she realized she had closed the door on her brother's finger, the middle finger of his right hand, which he was looking at like he was looking at a movie, which finger tilted off on a last tough thread of skin between the knuckles but was otherwise disconnected from him. The two siblings stood facing each other, on either side of what wasn't quite a closed door, and the brother's blood shot in a single pulse of his heart onto the chest of his sister's white dress and the girl could not understand, looking at the small touch of skin that kept the finger a part of her brother, how the finger could still be called a part of him, which was when the start of the new finger rose up from her brother's wound, pink and shining, small and boneless at first, looking like the nose of a mole, but then structured with bone, and becoming a brand new finger, and how, in the force of the pinching off of the sudden growth of the new finger, the old finger, her brother's original finger, dropped onto the carpet between their bare feet, no longer of use to anyone.

—

The girl Lila wrapped her brother's finger in a white handkerchief that her father had given her for her birthday and together with her brother she decided to bury the finger in the garden behind the house, the garden that had been their mother's responsibility when she was alive, the garden that was, now that their mother was no longer around, nothing more than a rectangle of black dirt, weeded over here and there. It made the girl Lila nervous to have an empty garden so close to the house like that, black with dirt, like a black swimming pool. She felt it was possible, though she knew it was silly, that open dirt so near a house, so forgotten, so untended, was bad luck for a house, as if the inhabitants of the house could walk out into the black dirt of the garden and be accidentally swallowed up by it, as if creatures could rise up from the black earth and themselves come loping into the house where she slept with her brother, right in through the kitchen. But something had to be done with the brother's finger and the girl Lila and her brother knelt on either side of the rectangle and the boy watched his sister cover the finger with dirt and he was happy to have her on his side in all of this, as Lila seemed like she knew what to do. And Lila saw her brother look at her in this kind and thankful way and she reached out across the small garden to touch her brother, to reassure him that she did know what to do, even though she wasn't certain that that was true, but then she saw her brother's blood on her white dress, and she looked at the boy's new finger there on his hand, shining in the moonlight, and so she said, without actually touching him how she'd meant to touch him, "We won't tell anyone about this," and her brother said to her, because he truly meant it, "I love you."

—

It was days and years that passed and it was a lot of time to the brother and the sister and the brother seemed again to forget that he was the Regenerating Boy, but the sister, Lila, could not forget it. She played with the few friends that she managed to have and she kissed rural boys that she knew to like her, but she could not forget about her brother, about how her brother had fallen from the window at her say-so, about how she had closed her brother's finger in her mother's closet door and the boy had just stood there and regrown his finger, like it was nothing, and she lay with her brother in the bed that they shared. She held his small body, which was no longer as small as it had been, and as the days passed and often through the night she felt his body grow longer and his skeleton denser, even as she held it all sleeping in her arms.

—

Soon the brother would be taller than she, Lila knew, and some nights she lay there with the mint and milk smell of her brother and she listened below to her father's voice as he entertained the series of women who might become their mother now that their mother was gone. The women of her father's would laugh and the women would moan and sigh and sometimes the women would climb the stairs to use the bathroom and the girl Lila would hear their footsteps in the hall before they slanted the door open and looked in on the brother and the sister sleeping, as if to see what all they, the women, might be walking into, might be getting involved with, with these two untended children, sleeping in the same bed, shirtless together, wrapped in each other's arms, motherless. And the women would look in on the shapes of the brother and sister sleeping and Lila would keep her eyes closed and she could smell her father on their bodies in the doorway and their father's liquor on their breath and she would keep her eyes closed until the women would fan back down the steps and it was always that they would never return, never return as anything, never return as mother, always that they would walk the gravel drive to their automobiles and drive away, leaving the father asleep on the couch and snoring, leaving Lila to fall asleep for real and dream about her brother.

—

She dreamed that she took pieces of her brother's body. She dreamed she watched his body grow back. She dreamed that she snipped him with snippers from her father's toolshed, or that she bit his body with the teeth of her mouth. She dreamed she took his finger and she would let the finger grow back and then she would take the finger again and it would grow back again and she would also swallow little bits of him. With the snippers and her mouth she took his toes, his ears. She dreamed that she took his nose, that she took his nipples, that she took the flesh between his legs that made him her brother instead of her sister. She dreamed she went further, chopping off his arms and legs with the bigger tools, stacking the large parts of him in the corner like wood, tossing the smaller bits into a tin pail that she carried with her down the steps, in her white dress, out the back door, to her mother's garden, where she knelt, again at the black edge of the rectangle, only this time in a dream, and planted her brother's body parts, in the open black dirt. She felt there in her dream, with her knees in the dirt, with her hands in the dirt, dropping the body parts of her brother into the holes she'd made, she felt like she was her mother there, or like at least she was her brother's mother, if not her own mother, and the next morning in the dream the garden would be ablaze with white stalks of her dreaming, and upon each white stalk a smoky pink flower, and she would cut the pink flowers from the white stalks and she would wind them into her blond hair, and when she saw her brother's face, looking out at her from the window of the upstairs bedroom of the dream, with his new body already grown back to himself, the look in his eyes told Lila how pretty and how strong he thought she was, and she felt strong, too, and it made her feel strongest to dream of taking her brother's eyes from his head, with her fingers, with a spoon, and she loved the idea of his eyes so much that once she scooped them from his skull, in the dream, she could not bring herself to plant the eyes in the garden, she couldn't part with them at all, they were like treasures, so that in the dream, while she planted her brother's other body parts, while she weeded to keep the weeds from choking the white stalks and the pink flowers, and while she harvested the pink flowers that bloomed out of the seed of her brother's body, she always kept one of her brother's eyes in her mouth, small and cradled on her tongue.

—

So often did Lila dream, like this, that it seemed it was no longer a dream, which she knew was dangerous. She knew, in fact, that she herself was dangerous, the power in her chest and legs, but especially outside of dreams. She would catch herself lying in bed with her brother's sleeping body twitching in her arms. She would wait till he was deep asleep. She would warn herself how it was all about to be a dream no longer, and she would lift his eyelid with her thumb, gently, to touch her tongue to the surface of his eye. On the first attempt, one night, she only allowed herself to touch her tongue to the white of his eye, in the corner of the eye. On the second, he had stirred in his sleep to feel her fingers on his eyelids, and he had said to her, "Quit it, Lila." On the third, she touched her tongue, as best as she could see it, down her nose, the tip of her tongue to the colored part of his eye, which part of the eye she thought might taste best, the soft looking brown she had seen almost all her of life, looking out at her from his face. On the fourth, she made her tongue a point and touched the tip of it to the black pupil of his eye, the part that looked like it was between her and the void of whatever it was he was dreaming. And on the fifth time, this time, her brother was awake, and he lay for her, uncomplaining, while Lila held him down at the shoulder and ran the rough of her tongue across the whole surface of his left eye, and then the surface of the right.

—

The knife Lila selected from the drawer in the kitchen of the peeling white farmhouse had a white bone handle and a blade so sickled and cruel-looking she almost selected another knife, so as not to scare her brother with the look of it, and she *would* have selected another knife, she thought, if not for the bone-handled knife's obvious sharpness and suitability. It was cruel-looking, she decided, but due to the sharpness it would be quick, it would be polite, and she carried the bone-handled knife at her side and pointed away from her body, as she had been taught with knives, and she walked up the stairs of the farmhouse toward where her brother lay sleeping in the bedroom they shared.

—

"What if you're remembering it wrong?" her brother asked. He asked this because he was younger than Lila and his mind had more easily forgotten the time when he had fallen from the window and broken his neck and the time when Lila had closed the door on his finger. But Lila knew she had not remembered it wrong. She sat pretzel style on the floor of the bedroom they shared and she faced her brother and between them was a white towel folded over on itself.

"I'm not remembering it wrong," she said.

"Or what if it was a thing that I used to be able to do," he asked her, "but now I grew out of?"

She nodded her head that this might be possible, yes, and she let him see her lay the knife on the towel between them and she crossed her arms. She said, "We don't have to do it," and she meant it when she said it, that they didn't have to do it if he didn't want to, but she also knew that her brother would do it. She knew that, for him, she was the scale and she was Lila. If he looked out at the silo in the cornfields she knew he would wonder to himself: how many Lilas is it tall? When he looked at the moon she knew that he wondered: how many Lilas could be fit inside of it?

"I'm not sure about it," said her brother, meaning the knife, meaning what Lila wanted.

"We'll pick something out," she said, "that you don't need so much. Not a finger, because fingers are more important. Not an ear," she said, "nothing that other people would notice you were missing, just in case I'm wrong, just in case it doesn't grow back."

"Like what?" he asked.

Lila uncrossed her arms and she picked up the knife again. With the tip of the knife she pointed to her brother's bare feet.

"Maybe a toe," she said.

—

Her brother lifted his foot and rested it on the folded towel between them, like Lila showed him. Neither the boy or the girl knew where their father was and they didn't care if they ever saw him again, though they knew they would probably see him again, with his beard and his eyes, with his stories about how their mother was everywhere in the world except for dead in the well out back, or at least they'd hear him snoring like a furnace in the house below them, hear his car in the gravel of the drive. The boy lifted his foot and rested it on the towel and the girl Lila rose to her knees, did it all quickly, like she had imagined it beforehand. She threaded the knife so that the unsharp top of it rested beneath the first four toes of her brother's foot, safe from the knife, but also she then poised the knife, at an angle, lifting the four safe toes slightly, so that the sharp side of the sickle, like a lever, touched the top of the smallest toe, at the base. His little toenail was so small it was barely even there. She gripped the handle of the knife in her left hand and with her right hand she made a fist and she hammered the fist down onto the grip of her left, and it worked even better than she had imagined it would work, and her little brother's toe popped off of his foot like a button off a coat.

—

After the new toe had grown back shiny and boned to her brother's foot, Lila sat still there on the floor and looked at it, at the new toe, for a very long time.

"What are you thinking about?" her brother asked.

"That toe," she said, pointing at the new toe, "is your toe, but it's also mine."

—

By the time it was fall and the moon went high and distant in the sky, a tiny white stone over the cornfields, Lila had taken two more of her brother's toes, the ring fingers on both of his hands, both of his earlobes (with her teeth), and his left nipple. And all of these body parts had grown back, softer even than new, had grown back belonging to her, grown back as hers.

—

By the time it was fall, the father hardly appeared in the farmhouse any longer.

Sometimes at night Lila and her brother would hear their father's car in the gravel drive, would hear their father stumble into the house, would hear their father enter the kitchen, then would hear him leave the house again, the headlights of his car making carnival shapes on the wall of the bedroom, and the brother and sister would descend to the kitchen, shirtless, after their father was gone, to find always a couple of bags of groceries on the kitchen table, fruit and powdered soups, jars of peanut butter, tough brown bread, and one time a can of condensed milk which neither of them knew what to do with and so spooned it to themselves in sweet globs. They would sit down at the table together and eat.

The girl Lila felt a growing sense of ownership regarding her brother's body and more and more she found herself wishing to take bigger and bigger parts of him, so that more and more of him belonged to her, and one night she found herself wondering, staring across the dark kitchen table at her brother while he poured honey onto the open face of a peanut butter sandwich, if his teeth would grow back if she removed them. The bones of his toes and fingers grew back, she knew. The bone of his neck had healed when he had fallen from the window. Would not then, also, his teeth grow back, if his bones did? Or were the teeth, she wondered, subject to different rules? She watched him stand on his chair and hold a piece of brown bread to his chin, as if it were a beard, and she watched him do an impression of their father. He stood on his chair to be taller, like the father, and he gestured this way and that, he made his eyes look stern and empty and he pointed his finger and gave orders. Lila smiled at this impression and she loved her brother. And what about, she thought, his internal organs? Everything, she imagined as she watched him, everything but the heart and the brain could be taken, and maybe even the heart and the brain, and she wondered for the hundredth time if she could get her little brother to hold still for her while she removed one of his eyes, as she thought often about his eyes, them more so than anything else, more so even than the teeth, and all of this imagining felt dangerous to her, like she worried that the specialness of her brother's body was changing her into something she would not have been otherwise. And she worried for him, too, worried for him at her hands and her intention, yes, and what she might ask him to do for her, but also for him in the outside world: what would other people do if they ever found out about her brother's body? If she, his sister Lila who loved him, felt the way she felt about her brother's body, which was that she wanted to see it taken apart, then what would other people, cruel people, curious and disinterested, feel about it? Would they come for him? Would they take him away? Would they cage him and study him? Would they hold him down and open him up? Would they ask the same questions she had asked herself about his teeth, about his heart and his brain?

—

The night before the day Lila would meet the boy named Jamie—an older boy from a village near the farmhouse, a boy who had blond hair like Lila's and who owned a big car—the girl Lila finally took one of her brother's eyes. She had not been able to keep from doing it. She knew there was a bottle of pink pills, belonging to the murdered mother, in the medicine cabinet of the upstairs bathroom. With this bottle of pills in her hand, Lila walked down the steps and she walked into the kitchen. She stood on a stool in order to reach the cupboard above the refrigerator and she took the bottle of brown liquor that she knew her father kept hidden there, and on her way out of the kitchen she stopped—she had imagined it so many times already—and from the silverware drawer she removed a funny spoon with a serrated edge, the only one of its kind in the drawer, and she walked with these things back up the steps to where her brother lay sleeping in the bed they shared together.

—

She held two of the pink pills out to her brother. She thought better of it, and she dropped one pill back into the bottle, and she held a single pill out to her brother.

"What is it?" he asked her.

"It will make you sleep," she said.

Her brother took the pill with no more questions and he put it on his tongue and the quickness with which he did this, with such trust in her, jolted through Lila's heart like a battery.

"It's stuck in my throat," the brother said.

Lila handed him the bottle of brown liquor.

"Just a couple of swallows," she said.

—

As her brother's breathing grew deeper she lay in bed next to him and she told him what she was going to do once he fell asleep.

"It will be just like the other times," she said.

"Why do I have to be sleeping?"

"It will be just like the other times," she said, "except it might hurt more." She said, "I don't want to hurt you."

They lay there like that for a while, side by side, and the girl thought she could hear the sound of coyotes off in the distance, and it was a wild sound. She waited until she thought her brother was asleep and she rolled over to look at him, and when she did he opened his eyes and from a dream he said, "I don't want to hurt you either."

—

She gave her brother another half of a pink pill and two more swallows of the brown liquor, and by the time he was unconscious the moon was high and tight in the sky, but it was still looking down at her, on a slant, this moon, through the bedroom window, like a witness. She straddled her brother's chest, keeping his arms pinned to his sides with her knees, and she used the thumb and forefinger of her left hand to open her brother's right eye. In her right hand she lifted the spoon and she touched the serrated tip of the spoon to the seam between the bone and the white corner of the eye, careful to make sure she didn't catch the eyelid, and she held the spoon there, visualizing the motion she would make before she made it. The small moon echoed back out of her brother's eye, like it had that night when he had fallen to the flagstones, and the girl Lila pushed the spoon in like pushing a spade into dirt, careful to keep the spoon so that it slid along the bone—she wanted the eye as whole and unmarked as possible—and, as she pried and pushed, her brother's eye moved loosely in his head, almost like it was struggling to get out of its own volition, and it was the only time during it all that she felt a little sick.

—

She placed the eye on her brother's bare chest and looked down at it and it was larger than she imagined now that it was no longer in the socket. She knew by looking at it she wouldn't want to hold the eye in her mouth, not easily, not like she had in the dream, when the eye had been smaller, and anyway outside the dream, in reality, she found she didn't want to put the eye in her mouth, not even if she could. It was not the same kind of eye. It was a real eye. It was both more beautiful and more terrible, and the brother had not moved at all during the process, and had hardly bled, and only toward the end, when she had had to saw through something tougher in the well of the socket, connecting the eye to the center of the brain, did he even make a sound. The sound was a sound in the bottom of his throat like he made sometimes when he was dreaming. She straddled her brother's chest more tightly and waited to see if he would wake up in the middle of what was happening to him, but he had not, and the eye'd slipped free and she laid his eye on his chest. She sat and watched closely the socket she had made to be empty, watched it for what she knew she was going to see, and it didn't take long, the new eye plumping in the socket like a cake in the oven, the firm of the white separating from the ring of the darker iris, resolving. She held the lids of her brother's eye open and she watched until the new eye grew in whole and seemed even to be looking at her and she felt in her chest something that was pride and heat and she knew that her brother would look at her through this eye and he would know that the eye he was looking through belonged to her.

—

The next morning at daybreak, while her brother slept through the mother's pills and the father's brown liquor, Lila rose early and put on her white dress and a coat over it for the weather and a pair of yellow boots and she went out into the garden, where she would bury the brother's eye in the hard black dirt. She could not see her breath yet in that morning but she knew it would only be a matter of time before she could. She dug the hole with the serrated spoon she'd used to remove her brother's eye and it was hard digging in the cold soil, and she placed the eye in the hole, the eye not looking up at her nor at the sky but positioned to look down toward the center of the Earth. And as she was covering the hole, she thought back to the night before, how after she had taken the eye her impulse had been to run away, to get away from her brother as far as she could, for his safety, and but at the same time how her other impulse was an impulse to stay and take the second eye, so that both eyes would belong to her, an impulse she fought until her brother mumbled in his sleep and rolled over and she knew that if she took the other eye, with him coming to like that, that she would hurt him.

—

As she tamped down the dirt over the eye and without being able to help it she thought of carrying the brown liquor to her brother again, this very same morning, carrying the spoon to him, shaking out pills for him, so that she could take that other eye, despite how she didn't want to take it, the eye that wasn't yet hers, and it was then that she looked around at the garden, in which she had buried so many of her brother's body parts. As in the dream she had taken to burying her brother's body parts in the garden, digging deep, packing down the holes tightly each time, the fingers, the nipple, the toes, now the eye, but this morning she noticed the disorder, the tracks in the dirt of the garden. Animals, she understood, had learned to come to the mother's garden at night—coyotes and raccoons, judging by the prints—to dig up pieces of her brother, who was the Regenerating Boy. At first this made Lila angry at the animals, like someone had stolen something from her, but then the feeling softened when she imagined the animals coming to the house at night, their sly movements, their gladness, and it only seemed natural to her, the right way of things, a harmony, and she no longer felt angry, but sad, sad for the animals. The country and everything in it seemed so hungry. She could feel the hunger in herself. And on her knees at the edge of the garden she was thinking about all this when she heard the horn of an automobile honking from the road.

—

With the spoon in her right hand and her brother's dried blood on the palm of her left, Lila approached the great green car idling on the road in front of the peeling white farmhouse. Against the flattened fields the green car seemed like a ghost of summer and the blond boy in the driver's seat smiled with too many teeth in his mouth and beckoned her to the car.

"Kind of late in the year to be planting anything," he said. He had been watching her in the garden. His voice was hollow sounding, like tapping on a false wall, and he was pretty.

Lila lifted the spoon in her hand and looked at it and hid it in the pocket of her coat. "I was just messing around," she said.

"I like your boots," the boy said.

She lifted one boot and then the other and she looked at them both. "I like them too," she said.

—

The boy's name was Jamie and he took Lila on long drives through the fields and sometimes he would park the great green car on dirt access roads and they would sit and he would talk to Lila about the city, a distant city Lila had heard the name of a few times before in her life, a city to which she had never been. The boy Jamie had been to this city. Or the boy *said* that he'd been to this city. He described tall buildings, he described the different colors of the people who lived there, he described it all in a rapid, glancing manner that made Lila think he might have been describing photos that he'd seen in newspapers or books.

"You ought to come with me," he said bravely.

"You're going?" she asked. She liked the look of his large hands on the steering wheel of the great green car, and when he looked at her like he looked at her she felt the same pride and heat she felt sometimes with her brother, but his voice had a hollowness that reminded Lila of her father. It was a voice that said the boy Jamie was hiding things, not so much from her as from himself, that he was his own mystery. Nor did he seem yet to know that she, Lila, was dangerous, and Lila knew this gave her an advantage, how he was not aware of who she was or what she could do. He thought of himself as smart, she could tell. He told stories of success in the city that she imagined would not come true, but still she liked his hands.

—

"I'm going to the city," Jamie said, "and I'm not coming back."

"Why don't you hold hands with me while you talk?" Lila asked.

The boy didn't look at her but he gave her his hand and she held it on her lap in both of her hands and she didn't think about her brother.

"You ought to come with me," the boy said again.

They sat looking up the access road toward the flattened fields across, and the girl Lila heard it in the boy Jamie's voice that he was afraid. She imagined, in the future, having to sit this boy down so that she could inform him what it was that he was feeling, when he was feeling it, and why.

She scooted over on the seat closer to the boy Jamie and with a hand she turned his face toward hers and she kissed him.

—

Another night the boy Jamie parked between the rusted-out silos of a farm that appeared to have been unworked by human beings for quite some time. There was a song playing on the radio that the boy Jamie thought was of some importance to him, and he turned up the volume and sang along with a look in his eye like he was already king of the distant city, and the girl Lila opened her door without saying anything about it and went around and climbed into the back seat of the great green car. The boy followed her, quiet now too and with a blank face, no longer singing the song that was important to him, and in the cold of the back seat Lila let the boy see her naked body. She hadn't known how far she'd let it go. The boy moved too quickly but she found she could control him with her hands, framed on his shoulders, keeping him bounded in like a horse in a stall so as not to let him spook. The song that was playing on the radio when they started was still playing when they were done and in the middle of it, with the boy distracted and closed off on top of her, without him even knowing it, the girl Lila ran her tongue over one of his closed eyes.

—

Later that night, or maybe it was another night, the boy Jamie pulled the great green car up the gravel drive of the peeling white farmhouse. The lights were off inside the house. Her father's car was not there, just as it was often not there. Lila held the boy Jamie's hand in the dark of the car and the lights from the dash lit their faces with upturned shadows.

"Out behind the house," she said, "there's an old field. Behind that field, there are some woods. At the end of those woods, there's a gravel road."

"I think I know the road," the boy said.

"My father won't be home," she said, "but all the same, just in case, through the woods is best."

"Okay," the boy said.

"Meet me on the road after midnight," Lila said, "and I'll go to the city with you."

—

The Regenerating Boy heard his sister's footsteps on the stairs and he pretended to be asleep because he didn't want to talk to her about what he wanted to talk to her about. He listened to her taking off her dress at the bedside, trying to be quiet, and he listened to her put on her pajama bottoms and she came to bed without her shirt like they had both done since they were small. Her body was cold and smooth and her body didn't smell like it always did. She smelled like Lila but she smelled like the boy in the green car he had seen sometimes in the driveway of the farmhouse and when she pressed her small breasts against him for his warmth something clicked in his chest.

"Father will be angry with you," he said to his sister.

"Father won't even notice," she said.

"I'll notice," the boy said.

"I'll come back for you," Lila said, and she tested the words she'd said out loud to the feeling in her heart about it, and she knew that she was lying, but she knew her brother believed her, she knew that he believed anything she said.

—

The boy awoke in the night with a panicked feeling he couldn't understand, a feeling that didn't seem to belong to him, a feeling that flitted around the room, like a bat. He awoke with his sister Lila straddling his thighs and the sickled knife was in her right hand. She was wearing her dress and her coat and her yellow boots. In her left hand he could see that she held in her hand what she had just cut from him, and between his legs he felt a feeling like lifting a cup of water to your lips and finding it the cup was empty. His sister rested the sickle knife on his chest and as usual there wasn't much blood and she leaned over and kissed her brother lightly on the lips. He knew she was leaving him. He knew she would come back for him. Between his legs he could feel a feeling like it felt when he slept wrong and his foot went numb. She said to him, "There isn't any moon out tonight." She said, "More than half of you belongs to me."

—

Lila left the knife there on her brother's chest where she had once also left his eye and in her right hand she picked up the small bag of her clothes and she went down the steps and out the back door of the farm house, holding what she had cut from her brother's body in her left. She had planned to bury it in their mother's garden, before leaving, like she had buried everything else she had taken from her brother, but she felt that if she stopped to take the time to do so she might never leave, never leave her brother alone, never leave the fields and the roads and the silos. So she walked past the garden and its bad luck and she walked past the old well where her mother's body was buried, and she could feel that her brother's eyes were looking at her from the window of the bedroom, that he had already healed from this new wound and forgiven her for it, that what was between his legs now was new and belonged to her, that one of the eyes that he looked at her with from the window was hers and belonged to her forever, and what she had cut from her brother's body she then pitched into the weeds of the overgrown yard, for the insects and the animals of the country, and her hand smelled like milk and mint, and she walked out into the empty fields and toward the dark line of the distant woods, knowing behind her in the window her brother looked at these same woods, the dark band of them floating in the distance, knew that he looked at these same woods and wondered how long would it take Lila to walk there.

ACKNOWLEDGMENTS

Thank you to the editors of the following magazines, in which these stories (sometimes in different form) first appeared:

Alaska Quarterly Review: "Death to the Daylight People"
Bennington Review: "The Regenerating Boy"
can we have our ball back?: "Easy"
The Fabulist: "We're Always Looking for New Blood"
Fence: "Afternoon with Supernatural Orphan"
Greensboro Review: "Trailer Park Gothic"
Hindsight: "We Hadn't Any Women"
Hobart: "Have You Heard from Our Assassin?"
Peach Mag: "The Ghost of Tracy Valentic," "Grant Proposal"
Quarter After Eight: "One Must Establish a Relationship with the Reader"
StoryQuarterly: "A Retired Witch," winner of the journal's 2023 fiction prize; thank you to judge Emma Copley Eisenberg

For all the suggestions and help: thank you to Jorie Graham, Sister Ashley Hudson, Kim Johnson, Case Kerns, and the atmospheric Binnie Kirshenbaum.
Thank you to Jordy Rosenberg and everyone at the amazing University of Massachusetts Press.
Thank you to Peggy Hartman for the map to the underworld.
Thank you to my current and former students at Harvard, Columbia, and the University of Iowa.
Thank you to Frank Bell and Susie Sharp for the support.
Thank you to Zoe, Marina, Griffin, Libby, Stella.
And to the elephants and the cheetahs and Jillian: love.

This volume is the thirtieth recipient of the Juniper Prize for Fiction, established in 2004 by the University of Massachusetts Press in collaboration with the UMass Amherst MFA Program for Poets and Writers, to be presented annually for an outstanding work of literary fiction. Like its sister award, the Juniper Prize for Poetry established in 1976, the prize is named in honor of Robert Francis (1901–1987), who lived for many years at Fort Juniper, Amherst, Massachusetts.

www.ingramcontent.com/pod-product-compliance
Lightning Source LLC
LaVergne TN
LVHW050959080826
845145LV00009B/2359

* 9 7 8 1 6 2 5 3 4 9 2 4 8 *